The Third Twin

John Rae

The Third Twin

A ghost story

Frederick Warne
New York   London

Copyright © John Rae 1980
First published in the USA by
Frederick Warne & Company, Inc. 1981
First published in Great Britain by
J M Dent & Sons Ltd. 1980

Frederick Warne & Company, Inc.
Printed in Britain
for Frederick Warne & Company, Inc.
New York, New York

Library of Congress Cataloging in Publication Data

Rae, John, 1931–
    The third twin

    SUMMARY: Shamus and his twin brother become
involved with a host of unhappy ghosts during the
night the boys spend locked in Westminster Abbey.
    [1. Ghost stories. 2. Twins—Fiction. 3. West-
minster Abbey—Fiction] I. Title.
PZ7.R123Th   [Fic]   80-16001
ISBN 0-7232-6192-X

The quotation opposite page 1 is reproduced by kind
permission of Macmillan Ltd, London and Basingstoke

"There is a widespread belief that twin children possess magical powers."
From *The Golden Bough, A Study in Magic and Religion* by J. C. Frazer

The Yoruba people of Nigeria believe that twins are spirits who have taken human form. They bring good luck to the family so they are given special treatment throughout their lives. If a twin dies a substitute twin is provided in the form of a carved doll. This 'third twin' is treated exactly like the living child. When the surviving twin is fed, clothed and bathed, the substitute receives the same careful treatment. If the substitute is well treated in this way the spirit will return to the earth.

Westminster Abbey

The first Westminster Abbey was completed in the year 1065. It was built at the command of King Edward the Confessor, the last Saxon king of England, as a church for the Benedictine monks whose monastery to the west of London (the Minster in the West) was one of the richest in Europe. Two hundred years later King Henry III demolished this Abbey in order to build a larger and more impressive one. It is Henry III's Abbey that we see today. It was opened in 1269 but not completed until 1502. Not long after, in 1540, the monastery was closed by Henry VIII. The monks were turned out and their Abbey became a Royal Church. The King appointed the clergymen to run the Abbey, a Dean and four Canons, known collectively as the Chapter.

What makes Westminster Abbey famous is the people who are buried there. It is also the church where the kings and queens of England are crowned but that doesn't happen very often. The dead are always there and their tombs and memorials attract millions of visitors every year from all over the world.

Edward the Confessor started it all. He was buried in the Abbey and when, in 1166, he was declared a Saint, his tomb became a shrine for pilgrims. When the Abbey was rebuilt, Edward the Confessor's shrine was given pride of place. Edward's successors as kings of England wanted to be buried close to this saintly man. So there they are: Edward I, The Hammer of the Scots, Richard II, who was murdered in Pontefract Castle; Henry V, the victor in the Battle of Agincourt, and many others.

It was not long before other people wanted to be buried in the Abbey. Sometimes the king himself insisted that one of his relatives or a man who had served him loyally should be buried there. One of the latter was Major John André, an English soldier in the American War of Independence. The Americans executed him as a spy but King George III thought him a hero and arranged for his body to be brought home to the Abbey.

But for most people it was the Dean and Chapter who gave permission. If the Chapter was short of money, space for a tomb was sometimes sold but more often the Chapter gave permission because the man or woman had performed outstanding service for their country. That is why the tombs of so many statesmen, poets and soldiers are to be found there.

The last person to be buried in the Abbey was the Unknown Warrior of the First World War in 1920. Since then the ashes of the famous have sometimes been placed in the Abbey but there is no more room for tombs. The Abbey is full.

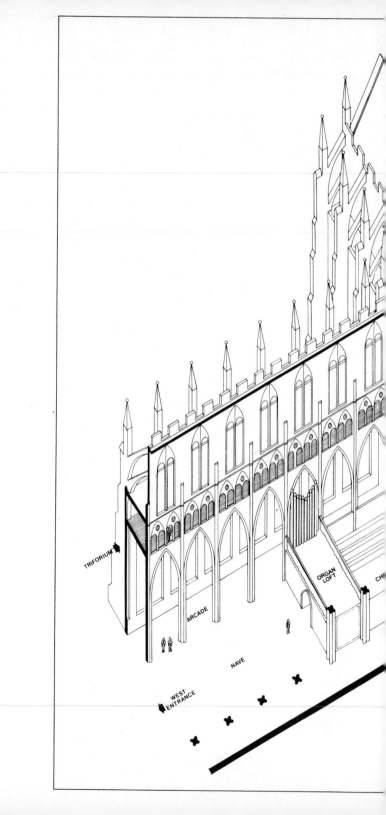

TRIFORIUM

ARCADE

ORGAN LOFT

CH

NAVE

WEST ENTRANCE

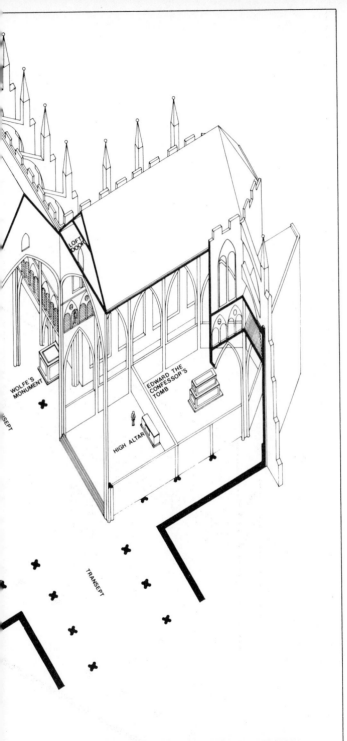

LOFT DOOR

WOLFE'S MONUMENT

EDWARD THE CONFESSOR'S TOMB

HIGH ALTAR

TRANSEPT

TRANSEPT

WESTMINSTER ABBEY

M.S. BLAIR R.I.B.A.

I was frightened. Not scared or anything like that. Just frightened.

We had chosen to sleep in the organ loft because it seemed safer up there, above the level of the tombs. It's not a loft really, just a sort of flat roof over the entrance to the choir-stalls. There's a curtain on a rail that hides the organist from the people in the nave on one side and from the choir on the other. It's easy to get up to the loft if you know how. The small door at the foot of the spiral stair is locked but the key is kept on a hook just behind the memorial to Isaac Newton.

There's a red carpet on the floor of the loft but it's worn and thin. I had only been lying down a few minutes before I could feel the bumps in the floorboards through the carpet and the nylon cover of my sleeping-bag.

Jonathan was frightened too. He was propping himself up on one elbow trying to look casual. But even in shadows it was obvious he was watching the curtain as though he half expected it to open the moment he closed his eyes.

'Lie down, Jonny,' I whispered. 'You're not scared are you?'

'Of course not. Don't be daft. What's there to be scared of?'

We both knew the answer to that. But I said nothing. Better not to mention them. I shut my eyes tight and tried to think of something else, but the word kept coming back, slipping in between one thought and the next. So I thought of an iron door and then slammed the door on the world but it came through the iron just as easily as if it was itself a...

'Are you awake, Jonny?'

'Only just,' he lied, and gave a pretty poor imitation of a yawn.

1

I didn't blame him. It had been my idea. 'It's the last chance we'll have,' I'd told him, which wasn't strictly true because the all-night opening of the Abbey which started the day after tomorrow was for the tourist season only, so we could try again in the autumn. But who was to say whether there would be another night when Mum and Dad were both away and Penelope left in charge.

Penelope hadn't put up much of a fight.

'If you're caught, I'll say I didn't know anything about it.'

That was all right by us. If you really must have an older sister, Penelope is the sort to have. She usually says yes in the end and she doesn't flap when things go wrong. She's not bossy either as most girls are.

Jonny hadn't liked the idea at first.

'Spend the night alone in the Abbey? Are you mad?'

'If you're afraid, I'll go by myself.'

That had worked because Jonny thinks he's a really cool customer.

So here we were.

Half an hour before the vergers closed the Abbey for the day, we had slipped out of sight behind the monument to General Wolfe, the madman who captured Quebec. I'd marked it as a good hiding-place a long time ago without knowing when it might come in useful. The monument was as high as a small house: on the front the General was dying in the arms of his friends but the back was just smooth stone and darkness. The vergers would never look behind Wolfe's memorial. They were old men and worked to a routine. In the morning they opened the Abbey to the public and in the evening they locked it up again. In between they kept an eye on the tourists and occasionally took part in one of the big services. When they had locked the Abbey they took off their black gowns and went to the Confessor's Arms for a pint of beer.

From our hide we could hear the vergers calling

goodnight to one another and then the echoing crash of the Great West Door being closed. We waited. The burglar alarms that rang in Cannon Row Police Station were being switched on. In a few minutes we had been sealed inside the Abbey as tightly as if we had been top-security prisoners. There was no way of getting out without setting off the alarms. At six in the morning the Night Constable would open the Great West Door and we would slip out into the spring morning.

'It's jolly uncomfortable,' Jonny complained, as wide awake as you please.

'Try lying on your back.'

'I have. It doesn't work.'

'Well, try again.'

I must have sounded impatient because he kept quiet for a time. I wasn't angry, just afraid of too much talking. Not that the Night Constable on his rounds in the gas-lit cloisters would hear us. We could shout and our voices would be swallowed up in the emptiness. It wasn't the Night Constable I was afraid of disturbing. It was the dead.

Now you see what sort of person I am. I said I wasn't going to mention them but now I have. Dad says self-control is the most important thing to learn; he says we have to have 'grip'. None of us knows exactly what he means but whenever we do something silly he just says, 'Grip, grip', and goes into his study.

I made a cradle for my head by interlocking my fingers and lay looking up at the Abbey roof. 'Grip, Shamus,' I said to myself, 'grip!' By the light from the street lamps in Parliament Square I could make out the pattern on the roof. Where the ribs crossed one another, there was a rose with petals of stone.

The Abbey is enormous inside. If you took the pillars away you could fit an ocean liner in easily. The building is shaped like a cross, with the High Altar at the head and the

Great West Door at the feet. Poets' Corner is one arm and the Statesmen's aisle is the other. Beyond the High Altar is the Shrine of St Edward the Confessor and beyond that again the Chapel of Henry VII. I know the Abbey pretty well. Dad takes us round every holidays telling us who's buried where and what they did. I quite enjoy that. The only trouble is that Dad always forgets what he told us last time so it can be a bit boring.

'What's the time?' Jonny asked.

I looked at my watch hoping it would be half-past ten, but it was a long way off.

'Half-past ten,' I told him. 'Go to sleep.'

It was only a white lie. I reckoned he needed it to be half-past ten more than I did.

Jonny and I are twins. We're not identical though some people say we look alike. I am seven minutes older than he is. Penelope says that if we were living in Italy that would make him the senior which doesn't make sense. I was born head first and Jonny feet first. That's typical Jonny. He's mad keen on football. He's bigger than I am and stronger in some ways. But I am more practical, I can get things done. Penelope says Jonny likes to have everything done for him and should have been born a prince. We will be twelve next July.

We must have been awake for nearly an hour after that. We didn't say anything, but you can tell when someone's awake: they're much quieter than when they're asleep. When I looked at my watch again it was only five to eleven. That really depressed me. If the night went on at this pace, morning would never come.

When Big Ben struck eleven, Jonny whistled through his teeth. He was no nearer being unconscious than I was.

'Do you know how many people are buried here?' I asked him, as he had broken the silence between us.

'No, and I don't want to know.'

4

I told him all the same.

'Three thousand.'

'You're making that up.'

'No I'm not.'

'Who told you then?' he demanded to know.

I couldn't remember. It might have been Dad or it might have been Algy Greaves, the Senior Verger, who always has something gloomy to tell you.

'Anyway,' Jonny went on without waiting for my answer, 'it can't be true. There isn't room.'

'There is if some of them are standing,' I argued.

'They can't be standing, you ninny, they're supposed to be dead.'

But I had him there.

'Ben Jonson is buried standing up,' I told him. 'He couldn't afford a big enough grave to lie down.'

'That's the only one,' he grumbled, but I could tell from his voice that he didn't want to go on arguing. Neither did I. It was asking for trouble to go on talking about *them*. I said, 'Let's try to get to sleep. It'll soon be midnight.'

Almost at once I started to slip away into that curious world that is between waking and sleeping, where daydreams and night-dreams mingle together and where you can guide your dreams through the currents, but not control them altogether because they are carried on a fast-flowing tide.

'Hey, Shamus!' I heard Jonny cry.

Wearily I half-opened my eyes. He was wide awake, standing looking up at the triforium, the cloister gallery that runs round the Abbey sixty feet above the floor of the nave.

He said, 'I've got a brilliant idea. We've never been up there before.'

'We're not allowed to,' I told him. The triforium was dangerous because there was nothing to stop you falling if you went too near the edge.

5

'Who's going to know?' he asked.

I shut my eyes again. He was too scared to go alone and I was too tired to go with him. But I must have been worried because it carried over into a nightmare. Jonny was standing on the edge of the triforium to show how brave he was. I wanted to shout to him to be careful but my jaw was all stiff. And then he jumped. I thought that if I was quick I could catch him but I couldn't do up my shoelaces. All the time he was falling, I was fiddling with the laces and the sweat was pouring off me. But then a funny thing happened. In the dream I said to myself, 'It's all right, it's only a dream', and the nightmare disappeared. I knew I was still asleep but I seemed to fall asleep again or to slip down to a lower level of sleep, like a shipwreck under the sea that is washed off its ledge by the tide and sinks into the darkness.

_____*Chapter 2*_____

When I woke I thought I must have been asleep a long time because I came up to the surface slowly. I lay still for a while trying to guess the time. There was no sign of the dawn though with the street lamps lighting the sky outside the Abbey it would be difficult to tell when the new day began.

Jonny was snoring. It must have been this that had disturbed me. Not that I minded. The worst was over.

I was so confident of this that I did not bother to check my watch when Big Ben chimed the hour. It was just a question of whether it was four in the morning, in which case I might doze off for a while, or five, in which case I would stay awake ready to shake Jonny in good time before the Great West Door opened.

But the great hammer went on striking – five, six, seven, eight. Something must have gone wrong with the clock's mechanism. Nine, ten, eleven – my heart seemed to shrink as though it had been squeezed by a witch's hand.

Twelve. And then silence.

'Go on!' I wanted to shout. 'Go on! Strike thirteen. Then everyone will know the time is wrong.'

It was so quiet outside as well as in, I could not have missed the thirteenth stroke if there had been one. So quiet I might have been struck deaf. I looked at Jonny. Was he snoring still? He was lying on his back with his mouth wide open as though he was at the dentist. There was no sound of late night traffic or of the swirling wind and spring rain that had been sweeping across Victoria Street a few hours ago.

So quiet and yet there was a strange stirring in the Abbey. No particular sound, nothing I could pin down, but I could tell that all over the Abbey, in the shadows and the half light, something was happening. I strained my ears to make sure I was not mistaken. It was like thinking you can hear before anyone else on the platform that a long awaited train is coming.

I rolled over and touched Jonny's shoulder.

'There's someone in the Abbey,' I whispered as he opened his eyes.

'Where?' he asked.

'Everywhere. Listen.'

It was louder than before, a low shuffling and murmuring but still without definite shape.

I wriggled out of my sleeping-bag and crawled towards the curtain.

'Don't look, Shamus,' Jonny hissed.

I lay still, my head close to the curtain, my right hand ready to draw the curtain aside.

The stirring was breaking down now into its separate parts, the footsteps and voices of a large number of people. The footsteps and voices seemed to be coming from all directions. I could not catch the words, even from those voices that passed directly underneath us through the arch and into the choir, but I could hear in the sound a note of anger.

I couldn't hold back any longer. I glanced at Jonny. He was still lying down in his sleeping-bag as though nothing extraordinary was happening. Seeing Jonny so casually unconcerned, I felt braver. I still don't think I was scared. I was excited. My heart was thumping away inside my chest and I was breathing quickly, but it wasn't like a nightmare where you can't even speak properly. It was more like the start of a race.

I moved the curtain. I was looking straight through the choir-stalls to the sanctuary steps and the High Altar. The whole area was crammed full of people. There were so many, it seemed pointless to be afraid of them. Who they were or what they were doing I had no idea. Some were in shadow; all had their backs to me. I supposed they were attending some sort of special service. That wasn't so strange. They have a service at midnight every Christmas and New Year's Eve. Just our luck though to choose this night to sleep in the Abbey.

It was odd that they had not put the lights on and that they were crowding forward instead of sitting down. Odd too that for a service their mood should sound so angry. But anything is possible in the Abbey nowadays. They had Indian dancers last year and then a jazz band with a singer who made everyone clap in time to the music. Mum walked out of that one.

I crawled back to Jonny.

'It's all right,' I told him, 'it's some sort of weird service.'

'Not in the middle of the night, it isn't,' he said.

'Why not? If they're opening the Abbey all night from Wednesday, it's almost their last chance.'

It was just then that the lights came on. They're enormous crystal chandeliers, hanging on long wires from the roof. They glow for a few seconds first and then burst into light.

I hurried back to the curtain and peeped out. The crowd was still pressing forward, talking, growling almost, but at nothing in particular, like a dog dreaming. They were all wearing the oddest clothes. I hadn't noticed in the half light. There were men dressed as monks in black habits and others wearing armour or chain-mail. There were men and women wearing long white nightgowns as though they had just got up from some old-fashioned bed, and there were others wrapped in bandages from head to toe as though they had been badly burned. A few wore red robes like kings. No one I could see wore ordinary clothes, ordinary for this day and age that is.

Then I saw something that made me shrink back. Just below me, dragging himself forward with his hands, was a man who looked as though he had been cut in half at the waist. A pair of legs, with trousers and boots, was strapped across his back like a big guitar. I felt sick just to look at him but the crowd took little enough notice, jostled him even. They had either seen him often or were too keen to get to the front themselves to care. It occurred to me that this might be a service for cripples like that one they have in France – where they all push forward in wheel-chairs and on crutches but only the lucky ones come away walking. But there were no other cripples I could see. The way most of them were pushing forward in the throng did not suggest they were disabled. They were all ages; and there were children too, some walking on their own, some carried.

After a few minutes, the crowd grew quieter and, apart from a few people on the edges, stopped trying to press forward. They seemed to be waiting for something or someone.

Jonny came up to my shoulder.

'Who are they?' he asked, more curious than frightened.

I shrugged. 'How should I know?'

One of the men in monk's habit stepped forward from the front of the crowd and began to walk up the sacrarium steps. At his appearance a strange silence moved over the people. I don't know why but I remembered that when a cloud crossed the sun my grandmother used to say, 'Someone is walking over your grave.'

The monk climbed the wooden steps to the pulpit. His cowl was down; from this distance he looked bald. He held himself with an air of authority and when he spoke his voice was deep and strong.

'My friends,' he began, holding both arms wide to include them all, 'we must resist now or we will lose our liberty for ever.'

_____Chapter 3_____

Did we know then, even before I had touched Father Benedict's hand, that they were all ghosts? Jonny says he knew all along. That's typical Jonny. He'd never admit he wasn't sure. But I cannot remember exactly when I realized. I think I said something like, 'They could be ghosts you know.' I was quite calm. One ghost would be enough to scare you out of the living daylights. But hundreds of ghosts are a different matter.

'They don't look like ghosts,' said Jonny.

'How do you know, you've never seen one.'

'Well, they're solid for one thing.'

All the time the monk was speaking, I was only half listening. Something about the Abbey being open all night and this being the end of what little freedom they had. The other half of my mind was saying, 'They can't be dead. Dead people don't walk around even in the middle of the night. They don't push and talk, they don't hold meetings and turn lights on. But if they're not ghosts who are they?'

'We could always ask them,' Jonny suggested, as though he had been following my train of thought. But I knew he didn't mean it. Jonny's courage is all proposals.

'No point,' I replied. 'If they are ghosts they'll disappear at dawn. If they're not we'd better stay out of sight.'

But even as I was speaking I think I knew that there was no 'if' about it. Very well, they are ghosts. I looked at my hands; they weren't shaking. I could talk properly. True, my heart was jumping still. I felt rather pleased with myself.

Yet, at the same moment, doubts came rushing back. These are ordinary people, strangely dressed for sure, but in every other way alive and solid. The last thing they looked capable of doing was walking through a wall.

I might have gone on speculating a long time, swinging from one opinion to the other, if Jonny had remembered to lock the door at the bottom of the stairs to the organ loft. He had not only left the door unlocked but wide open for anyone to walk up as they pleased.

The man who came up was Major André though we didn't know his name then of course. Jonny saw him first.

'Hey, Shamus,' he said loudly in my ear, 'there's someone to see you.'

See *me*! That's typical Jonny. He always eases out of things.

I turned sharply. A tall man in black was standing at the head of the stairs, one hand resting on the curtain-rail, the other holding a black three-cornered hat. His clothes belonged to some other time – high-collared jacket, red sash

11

round his waist and trousers that fitted his legs like stockings – but which time I could not guess. His dark hair was drawn back from his face and looked as if it might be tied behind his head.

He bowed slightly.

'We did not expect visitors,' he said in perfect English.

In the background, the monk was still speaking or rather answering questions because I could hear the different voices following one another.

I stood up. There was no sense in hiding any more.

'We're spending the night in the Abbey,' I said, surprised how easily the words came.

The man in black said nothing in response to this but studied us closely. Then motioning us with his hand to follow him, he turned to go back down the stairs.

We could have refused, I suppose, but somehow it never occurred to us we had a choice. Jonny let me go first. I kept a bit behind the man just in case. His hair *was* tied behind his head in a sort of pigtail; and his neck was wrapped in a wide, white cloth as though he was frightened of catching a draught. At the bottom of the stairs he turned right through the choir without bothering to check that we were following. One or two people were hanging about, detached from the main body of the crowd, lolling in the choir-stalls and obviously not much interested in what the monk or his questioners had to say. I didn't like the look of them. Their skin was greyer than the rags that hung loosely about them, and I had a nasty feeling that if you took the rags away you might find little more than bones underneath. Compared with these creatures, the man in black looked positively alive.

I closed up behind him. I wasn't so calm now and Jonny was walking on my heels.

The crowd opened grudgingly to allow us through. Close to, these men, women and children seemed much more hostile than they had appeared to us from the safety of the organ loft. They didn't say anything but they eyed us suspiciously and drew back as we passed. All the time we were walking through that dense mass of people I was aware of a curious sweet dusty smell that reminded me of the warm pinewoods in Portugal where we had spent our holiday last summer.

What they made of us in our shag sweaters, blue jeans and gym shoes, I could not imagine. The faces that watched us so intently gave little away. Some looked pretty shifty, I thought; others had the steady, level gaze of commanders and, unlike the crumbling figures we had passed in the choir, these men filled out their dark blue or scarlet uniforms. There was a boy of about our own age too. He was dressed like a prince in a historical play but the skin on his face was marked all over with dark, shallow craters as though it had been hit by a hundred bruising pellets. His eyes had an odd yellow glow.

The crowd was silent. The monk in the pulpit was silent too. I glanced up at him as we neared the sanctuary steps. He had a long, firm face and his expression was kind in a way that only firm faces can be. His white hair had been cut so close to his head it was almost invisible. When the man in black reached the foot of the sanctuary steps with Jonny and me in tow, the monk came down from the pulpit to meet us. I did not look back at the crowd; I was only too glad to leave them behind.

The monk held out his hand in greeting and without thinking I grasped it with mine. It was as cold as if it had come out of the deep-freeze ten minutes before.

He must have read the expression on my face for he said, 'Yes, we are all dead but you are warm and alive. Perhaps you can help us.'

I thought of the immediate things.

'You'd better turn off the lights,' I said, 'the Night Constable will see them.'

The monk glanced at the man in black. His eyes, I noticed, were very pale as though their colour had faded away over the centuries. The man in black shook his head, rather gingerly I thought. He pointed to the crowd.

'They will not disperse until they have an answer,' he warned.

'Then I shall tell them to be patient,' the monk replied. 'Plans take time to prepare.'

The man in black clearly did not think that would satisfy the hundreds who were already making their impatience obvious. They filled the whole space between the choir-screen and the sanctuary steps. Some were sitting now but most were still standing and pressing forward. The front row had linked arms like policemen at a demonstration.

'You will have to tell them something more definite,' said the man in black.

'I have already told them that we intend to resist.'

'They will want to know how, Father.'

'I cannot,' said the monk. 'We do not know. All I can say is that the Grand Council is to meet immediately and that we have the good fortune to have two living souls who came without our seeking and who might be able to help us.'

I could see that the man in black was still not convinced. So could the monk, for he added, 'We have no choice. If we don't start soon we shall have no plans by sunrise.'

He turned to Jonny and me.

'What are your names?'

'I'm Shamus. He's Jonathan.'

He climbed back into the pulpit. The cheer that greeted

14

his reappearance was half-hearted, and mixed with more angry sounds.

'We have six hours before sunrise,' he said, lifting his powerful voice over their ragged cheers like an eagle beating its wings into the sky. 'God has sent us help in these two young masters, Shamus and Jonathan. We did not seek this encounter with living souls; there is no blame in it for us. We shall turn off the lights now; we do not want to be driven back to our tombs before our plans are ready. Be cheerful. Lower your voices. Take your recreation as usual. Have no fear, we shall not surrender. The Grand Council will call you together again before dawn.'

For a moment or two it looked as though he had failed. The crowd swayed this way and that, but showed no sign of breaking up. The monk was master of the situation.

'Major André,' he called, 'the lights!'

It was just what was needed. Major André sprang forward and down the sanctuary steps. The crowd had no choice but to make way for him and in doing so began to break up. By the time he had reached the light-switches beneath the organ loft, the mass had already broken into groups which were moving away from the pulpit towards the transepts and the nave.

The lights went out.

As my eyes got used to the half-light again I found I could see the ghosts settling down to what I supposed was their nightly routine. The older ones sat together. The middle-aged walked up and down in twos and threes, their hands behind their backs, their heads bowed most of the time but raised occasionally to look up at the walls and pillars as though the aisles were paths through the woods and they were anxious not to miss the first signs of spring. The younger children ran about chasing one another; the older ones stood in groups looking bored. I wished Jonny and I could have called to them. We knew some good things to do.

15

'The Grand Council is meeting now,' said the monk.

Four or five other figures had gathered in front of the High Altar.

I said to Jonny, 'Coming?'

'Why not?' he answered cheerfully.

I felt compelled to whisper, 'Be careful.' But his only response was, 'We'll be famous.'

That's typical Jonny. He has this thing about being famous. He's going to run in the Olympics and play football for England.

The Grand Council meeting – which wasn't so grand as it was only nine people including Jonny and me – was held in the Chantry Chapel above the tomb of Henry V. You go up a winding stone stair that is so narrow and steep it's like climbing up a corkscrew. There are stone benches on three sides of the Chapel.

Jonny and I sat on one side with the monk and Major André.

'I will explain our problem,' said the monk as Major André was lighting the two candles on the altar.

'We know the problem, Father,' said the man sitting directly opposite me. He was younger than Dad and wore a long cloak of crimson velvet. He sounded and looked like one of those people who are used to having their own way.

'But our visitors do not, Henry,' the monk corrected him.

'At least effect an introduction for us,' suggested a large-bellied man with a double chin and silver hair so neat and trim it must have been a wig.

The monk nodded. 'Very well.'

He put out his hand to touch my shoulder. Even through my T-shirt I could feel the coldness.

'Master Shamus and Master Jonathan, who are friends, I take it?'

'We're twins,' I replied, 'but not identical.'

'Twins,' he echoed thoughtfully as though it had some special significance. He took his hand from my shoulder and introduced the members of the Council.

'Major André you have met. On the next bench is Mr Fox – who reminds me that introductions are required, and Lord Francis Villiers. And on this bench in the crimson cloak is King Henry the Fifth who prefers to be called Lancaster, and beside him, Mr Jonson ...'

'Ben Jonson?' I asked automatically, remembering that he had been buried standing up.

'The same,' said the man. His hair was the colour of raw carrot.

Even this brief delay was too much for Henry of Lancaster. He jumped to his feet. 'If this is a council of war,' he said, 'it is no place for a penniless scribbler.'

'Sit down,' the monk commanded him, with such authority and yet without raising his voice, that to my surprise Henry obeyed. 'We agreed that the Council must represent all the interests in the Abbey,' he went on. 'You are not here as a soldier. You represent the Royal House, that is all.'

The monk's hand moved to the last member, a naval man for certain, his uniform being unmistakable for all its odd fashion.

'Admiral Shovel,' said the monk.

Trust Jonny to think it was a joke. 'Shovel!' he exclaimed, trying to disguise the laugh.

'Shovel,' the monk assured him. 'And I am Father Benedict.'

So there we were sitting by candlelight with seven ghosts who were as solid and wide-awake as you and I.

Father Benedict explained the ghosts' problem: if the Dean and Chapter opened the Abbey all night to the tourists as they were planning to do, the ghosts would be denied their only time for recreation and exercise.

'We are allowed out of our tombs from midnight until dawn,' he continued, 'that has been the rule since the beginning of the world. Encounters with living souls are forbidden and punished by long delays in the consideration of your case. If we go outside the Abbey and deliberately seek an encounter with a living soul we will be sentenced to silence and darkness – that is, a long period imprisoned in our tombs without recreation and exercise. If the Dean and Chapter insist on opening the Abbey all night we shall be imprisoned anyway. That is our dilemma. Up till now we have been fortunate. Every night we have been free to take our recreation undisturbed. For the last four hundred years at least. When I was first buried it was not so easy. Our monks said their offices through the night in those days so it was a question of taking what exercise you could between compline and matins. But most of these people,' he waved a hand in the direction of the nave, 'have never known what it is like to be confined to your tomb for longer than a day.'

'We'll all learn soon enough, Father,' said Admiral Shovel, 'if we do nothing.' He was a short, tubby man with a broad, smooth face and a wig of black curls – not at all like an admiral, I thought.

'Just so, Admiral,' said Father Benedict unruffled, 'but the question is *what* shall we do.'

'Whatever we do,' said Major André, 'we shall put back our chances of promotion for a hundred years at least.'

'Longer, much longer,' was Mr Fox's opinion.

'What do you mean "promotion"?' I asked but even as I did so I could see that Henry of Lancaster was about to explode again. I could tell from the way he looked at me that he didn't like me. It happens like that sometimes; from the very first maths lesson I knew that Mr Askew didn't like me, and from the very first time he put me in detention I knew I didn't like him.

Father Benedict was watching Henry of Lancaster too as he answered my question.

'Promotion means you can leave the earth,' he explained, 'it doesn't mean you go to Heaven. It's just the next stage after here; you are no longer tied to the place where you were buried. The trouble is the Promotions Board is overworked. They're hundreds of years behind already. Only the earliest residents here have been promoted. If we seek an encounter with living souls our applications for promotion are put back indefinitely.'

'You shouldn't talk to us then,' said Jonny.

But Father Benedict replied, 'We did not seek this meeting. You came to the Abbey at night. Even so you are right. We risk some delay. But that is not the problem now. If the Abbey is open all night to tourists we shall be confined to our tombs twenty-four hours a day from spring to autumn. And who knows how soon the Dean and Chapter will decide to make it all the year round?'

At which Henry of Lancaster did explode.

'What, Father!' he exclaimed. 'Are we to be shut away like mad beggars just to please a rabble of foreigners? We have our swords. By God, there'll be encounters and damn the consequences.'

'That is easy for you to say, sir,' said Major André coolly. 'Your application for promotion has been rejected twice. You have little to lose.'

'And what of you, sir,' Henry retorted, 'what hope have you? A spy, a hanged man, a common felon. I have

19

hanged better men than you without noticing the time of day.'

'Which is why your applications are rejected,' Father Benedict reminded him.

Now one of the things I like doing is to settle an argument. Mum calls me the peacemaker of the family. I don't like it when she calls me that because Jonny always laughs and anyway 'peacemaker' sounds a bit feeble. But I like quarrels less.

So I had a go. 'Jonny and I could talk to the Dean,' I suggested, 'he's our godfather.'

'It's too late for that, I think,' said Father Benedict.

Mr Fox stirred himself. He cleared his throat, drew in a deep breath and began to address us all as though we were an audience of two hundred.

'We are dealing with two tyrannies,' he said, 'the tyranny of the Promotions Board' – and here he gestured with his chubby hand towards the Abbey roof – 'and the tyranny of money. If we challenge this wicked restriction on our liberty our chances of promotion are gone – who knows, perhaps for a thousand years. But if we do not, we condemn ourselves to months of imprisonment, without light, without exercise, without conversation, without all that makes death bearable.'

'What would you have us do then, Charles?' Admiral Shovel inquired.

'Do? I would defy both tyrannies. Loss of liberty is more terrible than silence and darkness in perpetuity. If the Dean and Chapter want to swell their money-bags by all-night opening, then they will have to do it ...' he paused to chuckle deeply at the thought of what he was about to say, 'they will have to do it over our dead bodies. I say defiance!'

I glanced at Jonny. He was miles away, scoring goals for England I shouldn't wonder.

A strange, lisping voice said in a roundabout way that its

owner agreed with Mr Fox. It was the first time Francis Villiers had spoken. I liked his face even if it was really too beautiful for a man. He looked like a young film star. His fair hair was so long its curling ends just rested on his shoulders. Even if Father Benedict had not given him his full title I think I would have guessed he was an aristocrat. He had that same look of lazy superiority you can see on Jonny's face sometimes when he's daydreaming.

'That makes three in favour of defiance to the living souls,' said Ben Jonson, 'then let me cast my vote against.'

The look on Henry's face was just the same as Mr Askew's when I can't answer one of his questions in mental arithmetic. I hate mental arithmetic. Mr Askew always picks on me because he hopes I will start crying. But I don't cry any more. I just stare back at him. One day that stare will kill him.

I half expected Henry to use Mr Askew's favourite phrase when someone gets the answer wrong: 'You do surprise me, Shamus, you really do.' But he just fixed Ben Jonson with a contemptuous eye.

'Three to one,' said Father Benedict.

'Three to two, Father,' Major André corrected him.

That did surprise me. I thought Major André would have been for defiance.

'Three to two,' Father Benedict repeated. He looked at the Admiral.

'Sir Cloudesley?'

The Admiral returned his look a full five seconds before replying.

'All my life I have taken risks, but now you' – and here he glanced at Henry and Mr Fox – 'are asking me to wait another thousand years before I see my beloved wife and children again. It is a lot to ask.'

'You were lost at sea, Shovel,' said Henry, 'a pity you were ever found.'

21

'I wish I had not been,' said the Admiral evenly, 'I should not then have had to put up with your arrogance for close on two hundred years.'

He turned back to Father Benedict.

'Father, you have led us in all matters ever since I came to the Abbey. I will be guided by you.'

'No wonder your fleet ran on the rocks,' Henry sneered.

Admiral Shovel let it pass. I admired him for that and would have liked to say so. Perhaps he guessed, for when he caught my eye he smiled.

Jonny chose that moment of all moments to have one of his brilliant ideas.

'I know,' he said, 'we'll be hostages. You won't let us go unless they agree to keep the Abbey closed at night.' He looked around the Grand Council expecting applause.

It was a good idea. Much too good for my liking. I could see the look on Lancaster's face. He knew a nasty trick when he saw one.

I said, 'I don't know. It probably wouldn't work.'

And I was relieved when Father Benedict said that they couldn't possibly ask us to stay.

'You don't have to,' Jonny blurted out. Anyone would think he wanted to be a hostage. He told me once that he had a foolproof plan for escaping if we were ever taken hostages by terrorists but when I challenged him he said it was a secret.

'You don't have to,' he repeated when Father Benedict looked uncertain, 'we volunteer.'

That's typical Jonny. He's always likely to land you in an awkward spot.

Father Benedict studied our faces for a time. Then he said, 'If one of you agreed to stay, the other could take our terms to the Dean and Chapter. That way we would be able to present our case without a deliberate encounter with living souls.'

'And if they do not accept our terms, Father?' asked Admiral Shovel.

'God help them!' snapped Henry.

And us, I thought.

_____Chapter 6_____

'That,' I hissed into Jonny's ear as we followed the ghosts down the spiral stair, 'was a bloody silly idea.'

I have to swear at Jonny occasionally or he never takes anything seriously.

The Abbey seemed lighter now. It might have been the moon shining in or just my eyes getting used to the shapes and shadows. There was less of a jostle in the transepts. Ghosts were still walking up and down talking though what they found to say to one another every night for all those years I could not imagine.

Father Benedict made his way to the pulpit. He was going to tell them that with the help of a hostage they might yet persuade the Dean and Chapter to cancel the all-night opening of the Abbey. But the more I thought about the plan the less I liked it. If I went out to bargain with the Dean and Chapter, who would believe me? If I stayed behind as a hostage, what would happen to me if Jonny failed?

I said in a low voice: 'You can stay, Jonny. It was your idea.'

He shrugged his shoulders. I bet he was thinking of the moment when the Queen congratulated him for being so brave.

When they saw Father Benedict in the pulpit, the ghosts closed in so that in a short time the transepts were packed tight again. Apart from their clothes and the waxy whiteness of their skins they might have been a crowd at a football match. Whatever happened to the old-fashioned ghosts, I wondered, the ones who wore white and walked through walls. Perhaps they had never really existed except in ghost stories. Perhaps the truth had always been much simpler. The dead waited in their graves until it was their turn to leave the earth. Like men in prison they had a time for exercise, from midnight till dawn. At least the stories had got that right. They kept their shape too though I bet if you opened their graves you'd find only skeletons. The only thing that was spooky about them was that all their blood had gone. I felt sorry for them rather than frightened. It must have been incredibly boring just lying or standing in your grave all that time with nothing to do. I could understand why they felt so bitter about losing their time for exercise.

Father Benedict paused and the ghosts clapped quietly. It sounded like an unexpected shower of rain.

'Which of you will stay behind?' he asked, as the soft applause died away.

Jonny raised his hand. The applause started again and Jonny smiled.

That's how it was settled. Father Benedict came down the pulpit steps. The crowd started to break up. One or two ghosts came up to Jonny to shake his hand.

It was not yet two o'clock. Dawn, Father Benedict told us, was at a quarter to six. Since there was time to kill, he suggested we should find a quiet corner and run over exactly what I was going to say to the Dean and Chapter. We went back to the organ loft. Major André came too but no other members of the Grand Council. That was a relief; I had had enough of Henry of Lancaster for one night.

What Father Benedict wanted me to do was this. I was to see the Dean as soon as possible after the Great West Door was opened at half-past six.

'Just tell him what has happened,' Father Benedict said, as though it was the easiest thing in the world, 'and our terms for returning your brother from the dead. The all-night opening of the Abbey to tourists must be cancelled. Let the Abbey be open until midnight and again after dawn if they wish. Tell the Dean we cannot yield any further than that.'

It was obvious to me that no one would believe my story and I said so. But Major André was reassuring. When people realized that Jonny had disappeared without trace they would have to believe me. But I still wasn't convinced. Everyone would say I had been dreaming or that it was a joke. And when Jonny could not be found I would be blamed and told that the joke had gone far enough.

I said, 'I must have some proof.'

Father Benedict's answer was to dip his hand inside the neck of his habit and draw out a small gold crucifix. He separated it from its chain and placed it in my hand. He said, 'I have worn this for five hundred years. Abbot Kyrton gave it to me when I took my final vows. Tell the Dean that if he opens my tomb he will find the crucifix held between the teeth of my skull. When he sees that it is so he will not ask for further proof.'

Jonny took the crucifix from me and turning it over in his hands commented that it must be worth a packet. That's typical Jonny. He's always trying to find ways to boost his savings bank account. Mum thinks he's saving up to buy a bicycle, but I know he draws money out each week to buy sweets.

'But,' I said to Father Benedict, taking the crucifix back from Jonny, 'I don't know where you're buried.'

'The Dean knows,' was his reply.

He turned to Major André. 'Now John, will you give your hat for Shamus to take?'

'No, Father, I will give better evidence than that.' He

asked me whether I had a pen. I had brought a pencil and paper in the hip pocket of my jeans so that I could write down any strange things we heard or saw during the night. Strange things! My goodness! We would have a story to tell.

Major André wrote on the paper and handed it back to me. I read aloud what he had written: 'Major John André presents his compliments to General Washington and begs that, notwithstanding the circumstances of his arrest, he may be accorded the privilege of a soldier's death.'

I looked at him. What did that mean? These were, he explained, the last words he had written before his death. 'I flatter myself that Washington kept my note,' he added, 'and that this copy in my own hand will be proof absolute that you have not been dreaming and that your brother is held prisoner for the time being by the dead souls of the Abbey.'

I folded the paper and stuffed it back into my hip pocket. As I did so I heard the siren of an ambulance approaching, growing in strength and then dying away again as the ambulance swept on its way down Victoria Street. That sound gave me a funny sensation. I thought I was alone. I looked at Father Benedict and Major André. They were still there. I looked at Jonny. He was there too. But I had this odd feeling that they were in one room and I was in another.

The odd sensation passed. I was too excited to try to sleep again so I left Jonny arguing with Father Benedict about which tomb he should be hidden in during the day and went down to the nave with Major André. He was a good guide. I wish I could tell you about all the people we met but it is only the odd ones that stick in the mind. Like Lord Castlereagh who was trying to hang himself from one of the iron bars between the pillars. Major André took no notice of him, pushed him aside in fact as though he was a curtain, but the sight of that swinging body gave me the spooks.

'He does that every night,' said Major André, 'either that or he throws himself from the gallery up there. Some say he has a pistol in his grave as a last resort. Poor fellow! He's too mad to know he's dead already.'

There were other ghosts I would have been glad to talk to. Edward and Richard, the princes murdered in the Tower, were about the same age as Jonny and me. I thought they could tell us what it was really like being dead, but I did not want to ask them in front of Major André, and he hurried me on. The princes swept off their curious floppy hats and bowed. They had long fair hair like Lord Francis Villiers and it fell over their faces as they bent forward.

A khaki soldier came to attention and saluted.

'Good evening, corporal,' said Major André pleasantly.

Major André introduced him to me as the Unknown Warrior.

'Why you?' I asked, looking away quickly. Part of his face had been shot away and I didn't want him to think I was staring at it. He answered me in a strange, wheezing cockney voice. He'd give anything to be back with his friends in Flanders, he said.

27

'None of us wanted this posting,' he told me, 'but we wasn't given any choice. They dug four of us up and put us on trestle tables in this tent. Then at midnight – midnight, I ask you – this officer comes in blindfold. It was blindman's-bluff all right. We was all praying 'e wouldn't pick on us. When 'e touched my boots my 'eart really sank into 'em, I can tell you.' He turned to me. 'You can't fix for me to go back, can you, son?'

I shrugged. What could I do?

'He doesn't really want to go back,' said Major André.

'I do an' all,' the corporal corrected him. 'This is no place for me. This is for officers, this is. If it weren't for you, Major, I'd 'ave gone scatty years ago.'

'Well, don't do that,' Major André laughed, 'we've luna-tics enough.'

I hardly noticed that as the night wore on the number of ghosts dwindled, but when we went back to the organ loft there cannot have been more than a hundred around. I never saw a ghost actually open a tomb and get in. They were just there one minute and gone the next.

Then I began to feel dog-tired myself. I told Major André that I would go and lie down in my sleeping-bag for a while. Jonny and Father Benedict had gone. I wanted to wish Jonny luck but I couldn't raise the energy to go and look for him.

I lay down. I knew I should have asked where Jonny would be hiding just in case I needed to contact him. But sleep came too quickly.

It was long past dawn. The morning air was fresh with just a faint whiff of the river. The blue sky seemed to sparkle in the sunlight. The Great West Door was open and morning filled the Abbey. I climbed up to the organ loft. Jonny's empty sleeping-bag lay beside mine, but that didn't prove anything. I looked over the curtain-rail towards the altar and the transepts. There was no trace of the crowd that had filled the area only a few hours before. The April sunlight streaming in through the clear windows above the Royal Tombs picked out the dust in the air.

It occurred to me that if I went down there and shouted Jonny might reply, by knocking at least. But I found the iron gates that led to the Royal Tombs closed. There was probably a duty ghost whose job it was to see that all was back to normal before the night ended. I pushed the gates. They shook but did not open. So I shouted through them, 'Jonny, where are you?'

A hand grasped my shoulder. It was the Night Constable. He said, 'Your sister's looking for you.'

He turned me round and walked me gently but firmly down the South Aisle. 'I should give the Abbey a miss for a bit,' he said by way of conversation. But I couldn't do that. I had to be sure Jonny was still in there. If I couldn't be sure of that, I would have to believe I was going off my rocker imagining such things.

Penelope was waiting by the Great West Door. She said: 'You've got to come quickly. Mum and Dad are back.'

An ambulance went past, its siren sounding out of place on this glorious morning We turned into Dean's Yard.

'Did you tell them about the ghosts?' I asked.

She just nodded and looked away.

The milkman's float was outside the house. He was exchanging full bottles for empty in the cradle on the doorstep. Mum and Dad were standing on the pavement. When they saw me coming with Penelope, they ran to meet me. Anyone would think I was the prodigal son. Mum put her arms around me and held me tight. 'It's all right, darling,' she said several times. In the background Dad was saying the same thing only he didn't sound so sure about it.

Breakfast was rather a solemn meal. There wasn't much conversation but then there never is at breakfast. Whenever I mentioned the ghosts Mum and Dad glanced at one another as if they knew something that I didn't. I looked at Penelope and her expression said, 'The less you say the better.' Did they all think I was round the twist?

Mum looked really shattered so that I wanted to tell her not to worry. Jonny was all right; it was just a question of persuading the Abbey people to stop their all-night opening. The sooner I saw the Dean the better. I decided to say nothing more about Jonny or the ghosts until then. With parents you know when to keep quiet. Jonny and I talk about this sometimes. When Dad is in a mood it's like playing Russian roulette; you never know what to say because any word might be the one to trigger the explosion. When Dad does explode, it's usually me who catches it. Jonny has this knack of being out of range. Even if he's around, Dad's temper seems to miss him as though he had a charm or something.

Dad was sitting at the end of the table now with the newspaper unopened beside him. He was old suddenly. I had always thought he looked young compared with other boys' fathers but now he looked old. I couldn't tell whether he was in a mood or not, so I chewed in silence brooding on the question of madness. Do madmen eat toast and honey? Yes. Do madmen feel as normal as I feel? Yes. Then perhaps I am mad already, I thought. I shall be locked away in an asylum. I didn't know what an asylum would be like but I imagined it was a sort of old-fashioned boarding school, only worse. I would be bullied by the older lunatics and Mum would only be allowed to visit me once a month. Every time I said I had talked to the ghosts they would put me in a darker cell.

But then I remembered the piece of paper I had stuffed into my hip pocket, the piece of paper on which Major André had written his message.

'I wasn't imagining it,' I muttered.

'What was that, Shamus?' Dad asked sharply as though he'd caught me swearing.

'Can I go now?' I said, making it sound like he'd heard me wrong the first time.

They seemed almost relieved. I went straight to my room. Jonny and I share the attic room; from the window you can climb out on to the roof. As soon as I had closed the door I pulled the piece of paper from my hip pocket and unfolded it. My hands were shaking. If the paper was blank I was mad, no question about it.

The writing was in pencil and looked faded as though the paper had been in my pocket a week or so, not just a few hours. But the message could still be read:

'Major John André presents his compliments to General Washington and begs that notwithstanding the circumstances of his arrest he may be accorded the privilege of a soldier's death.'

I read it through three times. My hands were steady now but my heart was jumping. I folded the paper carefully, replaced it in my hip pocket and went downstairs. My father was on the telephone. When he saw me, he stopped talking and put his hand over the mouthpiece as though there were

31

some words inside that he did not want to escape.

I hurried off in the direction of the Deanery. The cloisters were already packed with parties of tourists. I slid along the wall and then cut across the crowd into the Deanery courtyard. The Dean's bell started the usual barking from Hadrian, a mongrel with a deep bark and a soft nature.

The Dean opened the door himself.

'Ah, Shamus.' He did not seem surprised to see me.

I said: 'Something strange has happened.'

'Come inside and tell me.'

The Dean is godfather to Jonny and me. We don't see him much even though he lives so close but there's one thing especially I like about him. He listens.

We went to his study. There were so many books they overflowed from the shelves on to the window-sills and the floor. There were books on the chairs, too, so that you had to move them, like cats, before you could sit down; and you knew that, like cats, they would be back on the chair as soon as you had gone.

'Jonny and I spent the night in the Abbey,' I began, thinking it best to get the illegal bit over first.

He's older than Dad and short-sighted and kind.

'I hope you were not disturbed,' was his only comment.

'Well, that's the point, we were.'

So I told him everything. His only interruptions were to clarify a fact or to murmur 'Oh yes' when I mentioned one of the ghosts by name, as though he was glad to hear that old so-and-so was still around. If he thought I was out of my mind he gave not the slightest hint. When I showed him the piece of paper with Major André's message he studied it carefully.

'Have you shown this to your father?' he inquired.

'No, he's in a bit of a mood, I think.'

The Dean nodded sadly. I thought I saw a tear shining behind his glasses.

'It was nobody's fault,' he said mysteriously.

'What shall we do?' I asked him. 'We've got to do something. We can't just leave Jonny there for ever.'

I didn't want to ask him straight out whether he thought I was round the twist but he got the message.

He peered into my face as though the clue to all the strange happenings was there if only he could recognise it.

'People have delusions, dreams that seem real to them, Shamus,' he said. 'It doesn't mean they're mad, it's more like a sickness that can be cured. Sometimes it's caused by an experience so powerful – a shock perhaps – that the mind can't bear to think about it as real; so the imagination takes over. It's as though the person had in his mind a magic charm that muddles up what is real and what is imaginary. Do you remember when we came to your Christmas Eve supper last year and we were talking about those machines that were used during the war for turning ordinary language into code?'

I nodded. Jonny had said he knew how they worked.

'Well, the human mind can sometimes work like those machines, translating all or part of what it sees and hears into a code. If it only translates part, then what is real and what is code get all jumbled. Does that make sense to you?'

'I'm not making it up,' I told him. I *knew* what had happened and I couldn't see why he needed any complicated explanations.

'No, I'm sure you're not doing that,' he said, 'but whether your story about the ghosts is true in fact or just in your own mind, I don't know.'

'What about Major André's message? That's a fact.' I held the paper up to remind him. 'And what about Father Benedict's crucifix? How could I know about that?'

'I agree that is a puzzle,' he said calmly.

'Why don't you look then, it would be easy to check?'

'We don't open tombs just like that,' was his reply.

'What about Jonny then? Where's Jonny?'

He stood up and went to the window, placing his feet in the spaces where the books were not without looking down. Above his head the great, grey buttresses of the Abbey stood out sharply against the clear blue sky.

'If you are right,' he said without turning to face me, 'and Jonny is a hostage of the dead, then he may be dead too. Had you thought of that?'

I sprang from my chair. 'Jonny isn't dead,' I almost shouted at him. 'He's unconscious, that's all. But if you don't agree to the ghosts' terms he'll be as good as dead because they'll never let him go. And then it'll be your fault.'

That made him think twice. When he turned to face me I could tell I was winning him over. He said: 'All right, we must help Jonny. If he is with the ghosts we will have to deal with them. If he's somewhere else ...'

'He's with the ghosts,' I assured him.

'Others may take some persuading of that.'

'I can persuade them. I have proof.'

Chapter 9

Dad did need persuading. He was all for calling the police. That's typical Dad. He's got both feet on the ground. I can hear his voice now: 'There's always some perfectly simple explanation,' he says whenever anything mysterious crops up. Dad doesn't believe in God so you can hardly expect him to believe in ghosts.

He wasn't really angry with me. He seemed more angry with Jonny, though it was Jonny we were all worried about.

'Why on earth did he do such a crazy thing?' he asked,

not expecting anyone to answer for he went on talking straightaway. 'He must have known it was dangerous. He must have known. It was a stupid thing to do.'

'It was his idea,' I said defensively.

We were sitting in the kitchen. The Dean had brought me home and told Mum and Dad everything. At first Dad thought Jonny and I were up to some practical joke; then he thought that we were trying to cover up something we had done wrong. But the Dean told him that he must not rule out the possibility that I was telling the truth.

'What the truth means,' he added, 'I don't know. We can't believe it literally of course but then perhaps we're not supposed to. Perhaps it's just a clue or series of clues to what has happened to Jonny.'

'All right. I accept that,' Dad placed both his hands on the table palms down as he was speaking. 'I accept that Shamus *thinks* he is telling the truth. But whatever happened to Jonny is real not imaginary.'

Mum took my hands in hers.

'Darling, you're sure Jonny isn't hurt?'

'He's not *hurt*,' I replied, 'but he is unconscious. He must be because he's in one of the tombs.'

There was a pause. Penelope put cups of coffee on the table. Dear Penelope, she's super. I think she was the only person who didn't secretly think I ought to see a head-shrinker.

'Wherever he is,' said Dad, 'I insist we call the police.'

I stood up to him then. I said, 'It isn't for the police, Dad. Jonny hasn't run away. He's a hostage and the only way we'll get him back is if the Dean cancels the all-night opening of the Abbey.'

When nobody said anything to that I was encouraged to be braver.

'If you think I'm suffering from shock or something, why don't you check on Major André and Father Benedict?'

To which Mum said, 'Darling, if we promise to do that, or at least to try, will you rest for a while? I'll ring Dr Anderson. It won't do any harm for him to look at you. It's just another check we ought to make.'

I looked at the Dean. Would he open Father Benedict's tomb? I could trust him to give a straight answer.

'It's not my decision,' he replied, 'I shall have to consult the Chapter. But I shall try to persuade them to agree, not because I expect to find Father Benedict's crucifix between his teeth as you describe, but because not finding it might help you to remember what really did happen.'

'And I will check Major André's message,' said Dad, picking the piece of paper off the table with his forefinger and thumb as though it was radio-active.

'How, Dad?' I could have hugged him for saying that but I had to be sure he wasn't fooling. That's the trouble with Dad. You can never tell when he's serious.

He said he would send a telex to the National Library in Washington; if Major André's note to General Washington existed they would know.

'Major John André, Adjutant General to the British forces in America,' said the Dean thoughtfully. 'It's coincidence, of course, and not significant but we were talking about restoring his monument the other day. The head is missing.'

Dad asked what happened.

'To the head?'

'No, Major André.'

'He was hanged as a spy at the age of twenty-nine,' the Dean explained. 'He was caught behind the American lines in civilian clothes. He claimed a soldier's right to be shot but Washington refused.'

I remembered the white scarf and the head gingerly turned.

I could see that what the Dean had said upset Dad. He stood up, jarring the table.

'I'll telephone the police,' he said, bringing us all down to earth.

I flopped on to my bed without taking my gym shoes off. Mum had drawn the curtains as though the sunshine would make me worse. I couldn't sleep – I kept thinking of Jonny. Was he able to think while he was in the tomb? Or would he just wake up at midnight like the other ghosts?

Dr Anderson came. He's a real creep. He has this bedside manner that makes you want to throw up. He doesn't whisper exactly but he talks quietly the whole time as though you are some sort of nut-case.

'What seems to be the matter?' he said softly, sitting on the side of my bed and reaching forward to take my pulse.

'Nothing,' I told him.

He nodded.

'Any pain?'

'No.'

'Dizzy?'

I shook my head.

He pushed up my T-shirt and knocked on my chest in one or two places. Then he felt my forehead and under my jaw.

He sat back.

He said: 'Well, young man, what's your game?'

When you're eleven and someone calls you 'young man' you know at once to be on your guard. I glared back at him wondering whether he was worth having an argument with.

He spoke to Mum who was standing at the end of the bed, but kept his eyes on me.

'He could be suffering from shock,' he said, 'the pulse is slow. But as for his hallucinations, there's nothing here to account for them.'

He stood and mentioned the name of a specialist that

Mum might like to call. She said she would think it over.

Left alone I began to feel really depressed. It's no joke thinking you may be going mad. I had to keep reminding myself of Major André's note. That was the only proof that I wasn't crazy or suffering from the effects of shock. But I wondered about that shock idea all the same. I'd read about soldiers who had been shell-shocked in the First World War – they had lost their memories and even believed that they were someone else.

In half an hour or so the mood of depression disappeared, just fell away of its own accord. I cracked back the curtains. The sun blazed like midsummer. To hell with doctors. With all their mumbo-jumbo and soft voices they couldn't help Jonny. But I could. I could rescue him on my own if it came to that.

That's the sort of person I am. I can be feeling right down in the dumps one minute and ready to take on the world the next. A wave of excitement flows through me as though someone had switched me on. Then I believe I can do anything.

If the Chapter refused to open Father Benedict's tomb and Dad failed to get anything out of Washington, then I would go back to the Abbey tonight. I would tell the ghosts' Grand Council that the deal was off. I had done my best. Now they would have to sort out their quarrel with the Abbey without our help. We had volunteered so we could pull out when we wanted. If the ghosts were difficult, well then, Jonny and I knew a trick or two.

I told Mum I was feeling better.

'Where are you going, darling?'

I could see from her eyes that she had been crying. She was doing the ironing.

'Nowhere in particular,' I replied.

I asked where Dad was.

'He's at the office sending a telex.'

She rested the iron on its heel. 'He's doing all he can, darling.'

'Did he call the police?'

'He went to see them. He had to fill in a missing persons' report.'

'Don't cry, Mum. Jonny'll be all right. I know he will.'

I made straight for the Abbey. The spring sunshine was so unexpected after the weeks of high wind and sweeping rain that people stopped in the street and looked up at the sky as though they did not trust winter to have surrendered at last.

Tourists flowed in and out through the Great West Door. Everywhere, it seemed, there were placards announcing that tomorrow the Abbey would be open all night; and for every night until the end of September. The placards were headed 'Pilgrims' Festival'. I had read the announcement often enough. 'In response to the overwhelming demand from the peoples of the World, the Dean and Chapter have agreed that the Abbey shall be open all night during the summer months. Pilgrims will be able to visit the Shrine of St Edward and the other Royal Tombs at any time except when divine service is being held.'

I didn't think anyone was taken in by all that stuff about pilgrims. The Abbey needed the money; so did the Tourist Board. It was a deal between them. But Jonny's life was worth more than all the wealth the tourists would bring.

I followed a group of Japanese into the Abbey. I didn't have a plan exactly but I thought that if I visited the most likely tombs he might have left a sign.

Mr Ridley, the caretaker, emerged from the shadow of his office and grasped my arm.

'Don't you dare do that again,' he warned.

He was a short man with jet-black hair and breath that always smelt of whisky.

'What?' I asked him as the tourists flowed round us like water round a piece of driftwood caught by the rock.

'What! What! You know what,' he barked, turning his shoulder to me and edging away between the rows of chairs. I supposed he must be talking about our staying the night in the Abbey but he hadn't finished.

'I'm not responsible,' he told me. 'If you go up there without permission then it's your responsibility. Is that clear?'

'Quite clear,' I assured him. What on earth was he talking about?

He seemed to be edging away again but he stopped and raised his voice so that the tourists turned to see what the fuss was about.

'It's you who's responsible,' he said, 'no blame falls on me; not in the middle of the night it doesn't. Make no mistake about that.'

He went at last, shaking his head from side to side with such exaggeration you would have thought the blame was still clinging to his hair.

I moved on to start my check of the likely tombs. I know the Abbey pretty well thanks to Dad's tours and I can tell you where almost anyone is buried.

Henry of Lancaster is buried behind the shrine of Edward the Confessor. It's a plain tomb with a wooden effigy of Henry lying on top. That effigy is really flattering; it makes Henry look as if he was a gentle, modest sort of person.

I knocked on the side of the tomb. I couldn't see any sign of Jonny and I thought it just possible he would reply to my knocking if he was inside. I felt a bit of a charley knocking on Henry's tomb but it was the most likely place. For one thing there was clearly room for more than one person inside. But there was no answer. Knowing Jonny, he was more than likely to be asleep.

The other tombs were less promising. Lord Francis Villiers was buried in the same tomb as his father, the Duke of Buckingham, together with heaven knows how many brothers and sisters. There might have been room for one more but I doubted it. There was certainly no room in the narrow hole where poor Ben Jonson had to stand all day. I tried Mr Fox in the North Transept but there was no way of knowing how large the grave was beneath the black marble slab. I sat in one of the wooden chairs and tried to slip inconspicuously to my knee. The black marble felt solid and I was pretty certain my knocking could not have been heard within.

'That's why the triforium is out of bounds.'

It was Mr Ridley again. I smelt the whisky before I heard the words.

'It's to stop lads like you larking about,' he went on as I struggled to my feet in the narrow space between the chairs. 'If I was your father I'd know what to do.'

'But you're not,' I reminded him.

'I'm glad of that, I can tell you,' he said, and laughed at his own wit as he stood there swaying like a piece of dark seaweed in the tourist tide.

I pushed past him and made for the other side of the Abbey where Admiral Shovel was buried.

Admiral Sir Cloudesley Shovel is buried near the East Cloister door and Major André is only a few yards away.

41

The trouble in both cases is that the white marble memorial on the wall suggests a large grave but the small black lozenge in the floor suggests that at best they occupy one coffin's worth and none to spare. My thoughts turned to Father Benedict. In a way his was the most likely tomb but I had no idea where it was. Apart from the Abbots, the Benedictine monks had no memorials. Yet Father Benedict had said that the Dean would know where he was buried.

I saw Mr Ridley talking to one of the vergers. At the risk of receiving another blast, I went up to him and with as much politeness as I could raise (which is quite a lot when I want something badly) asked if he knew the tomb of Father Benedict.

I should have known better.

'You're a cool one,' he said, clearly not meaning it as a compliment, 'your parents sick to death with worry and you come along with this cock and bull story about ghosts. Well, there'll be no graves opened while I'm caretaker.'

He must have seen that I was not much impressed by this for he added, 'There's a name for boys like you,' though I was pretty sure he couldn't have told me what it was if I'd asked him.

I did not lose hope. If the Dean knew where Father Benedict was buried he would tell me.

I ran into Penelope in Dean's Yard.

'Shamus, I've been looking for you.'

'I've got a lot to do,' I said in case she had a job for me.

'Daddy's heard from Washington.'

Where was I standing when she told me that? I want to remember exactly how I felt and what I could see. It's raining in Dean's Yard today but that day the spring sunshine made Penelope screw up her eyes when she talked to me. She said, 'You were right – word for word. They're sending a copy so that we can check Major André's handwriting.'

In the Deanery drawing-room a meeting was being held. I could imagine what they were talking about. Dad and the Dean were sitting on the sofa. Mr Bullstrode, the Collector, was standing with his back to the empty fire-place. He's the Abbey's public relations man; he organises their money-raising and it was his idea to open the Abbey all night to the tourists. Dad says he's the Abbey's hatchet man; he does the dirty work the clergy don't want to touch.

In the two armchairs sat a policeman whose uniform and silver pips suggested a senior rank and an elderly clergy-man who turned out to be the Church of England's expert on the supernatural.

Dad sprang up as I entered and put his arm round my shoulder.

'I've got news for you,' he said.

'I know. Penelope told me.'

I was feeling on top of the world. 'Will you open the tomb now?' I asked the Dean.

He said, 'You know Mr Bullstrode, the Collector? This is Chief Inspector Dawkins of Scotland Yard's Special Crimes Squad, and Canon Ambrose who is the Church of England's authority on ... well, what would you say, David?'

'Ghosts,' the Canon replied simply and smiled at me.

I said, 'Hallo,' while by the fire-place the Collector breathed out sharply through his nose like a steam-engine ready to depart.

'Do *you* believe me?' I asked the Canon.

'In the matter of ghosts,' he replied, 'I have found it best to rule out every other possibility first. Ghosts exist, if at all, by a process of elimination.'

This reply met with a general murmur of agreement.

I looked at Dad.

He said, 'If Major André's handwriting matches that on the note you found in your pocket, then I think we should take the next step and open Father Benedict's tomb. But we shall not have the copy over the wire from Washington for an hour or two. Until then we must explore other possibilities.'

The Dean nodded. The steam-engine by the fire-place hissed impatiently but did not move. It was Dad who explored the other possibilities.

'Shamus, think back,' he urged, 'what time did you and Jonny go into the Abbey?'

'Just before it closed,' was my reply.

'Did you go straight to the organ loft?'

'No, we hid behind General Wolfe with our sleeping-bags. When the vergers had all gone we came out.'

'What happened then?'

I hesitated. I could not remember exactly how we had filled the time until it was worth trying to go to sleep.

I said, 'I think we just mucked about until it was dark.'

'Then you went up to the organ loft?'

'Yes.'

Dad leaned forward. 'Now think carefully,' he said. 'Did Jonny go to sleep before you or did you go to sleep before him?'

'I think I went to sleep first. He was talking about exploring somewhere.'

'So he could have left the organ loft while you were asleep?'

'But he was there when I woke up,' I reminded him.

'No, he wasn't, Shamus, that's the point. When you went back to the organ loft in the morning he had gone.'

'I meant when I woke up during the night.'

'*If* you woke up during the night,' said Canon Ambrose gently.

I realised then that even Major André's message had not

44

persuaded them. I should have brought his hat as well. I felt like telling them they didn't care a damn what had happened to Jonny.

The Dean understood. He said, 'We all want Jonny back safely. Your mother and father want that more than anything else in the world. But we don't know where to start. What you have told us is very strange. But we haven't ruled it out. That's why I asked Canon Ambrose to come. He knows that stories of the supernatural can sometimes be a clue to something that has really happened. He is helping us try to interpret your story. But as your father says, we must follow up other possibilities. It's possible Jonny left the Abbey while you were asleep and somehow avoided setting off the alarms. It's even possible – though I must say I think it unlikely – that he has been kidnapped. As Inspector Dawkins knows, the Abbey has for a long time been a target for the IRA.'

I interrupted him. 'Major André doesn't work for the IRA,' I said. The Dean glanced at the policeman, needing support.

Chief Inspector Dawkins did not believe in ghosts. I could tell that. He never once referred to Father Benedict or Major André. But he was no thick copper, I could tell that too. He had the sort of face that was quick to notice things but slow to give away how much it had noticed. His fair hair was cut short and his blue eyes held you steady while he was talking to you.

He told me that Jonny's description had been circulated to all the police forces in the country. If Jonny was lost or being held hostage, he was probably still in London. Every police officer on duty in the metropolitan area would be on the look-out for him. The London evening papers would help too. Jonny's photo would be on the streets by noon in the early editions. It all sounded like a routine operation for missing boys.

I told him Jonny would never run away. He had nothing to run away from.

'You never know people,' he said, 'not even your twin brother. Something happens and they act differently from anything you've ever known. My guess is your brother has taken off for a lark and that he's now too scared to come home.'

'He's in the Abbey,' I said stubbornly.

'I think that's unlikely,' he said, obviously falling over backwards not to show that he thought I was daft. 'But ghosts are the Canon's business. Police deal in facts.'

'Major André's message is a fact,' I told him.

'It *is* fact, that is certain,' Canon Ambrose agreed. 'It is here and we can all see it. But seeing it and holding it in our hands does not tell us what it means.'

'It's your job to explain it,' I said impatiently.

'To try, Shamus, to try. I was a surgeon before I became a priest. I knew what I was dealing with then. But the supernatural is still an unknown country to us. We catch glimpses of it from time to time but we don't know what laws it obeys. We can't predict what will happen there and our best explanations of what has happened are just wild guesses.'

Oh God, I thought, he would change his tune if he could meet Father Benedict and Major André or see the nave packed with ghosts. I said, 'All the ghosts want is the time between midnight and dawn.'

That set Mr Bullstrode off. All this time I had been aware that he was building up steam. Now he cleared his throat with such an explosion Hadrian sprang up and ran barking at the door.

'Mr Dean,' he began in a voice that suggested he was with difficulty controlling powerful forces within, 'I am a patient man and I have listened patiently to all that has been said. There can of course be no question of cancelling the all-night opening of the Abbey. Let us be clear on that point. It will save unnecessary discussion. May I remind you that the official opening will be attended by a large number of distinguished guests including representatives of foreign governments. I would also remind you that the opening has been publicised in every country that could conceivably send tourists to Britain and that as a result we are anticipating a through-put of 10,000 tourists a night, give or take a thousand ...'

'Pilgrims, Mr Bullstrode, pilgrims,' murmured the Dean.

'Pilgrims, quite so, Mr Dean. And as pilgrims they will wish to enter the Royal Tombs for which the special over-time entry charge will be one pound a head. Allowing for expenses – staff, electricity and so on — we anticipate a net profit over the five-month period of something in excess of a million pounds.'

He paused to let the sum sink in.

'Jonny's worth more than that,' I said quietly.

He brushed me aside with a gesture of the hand as though I was an insect annoying him. 'Now, Mr Dean, as I say, I am a patient man. Out of respect for you and for his father I have listened to this boy exercising his imagination but I do not propose to waste any more time on the interesting subject of ghosts.'

He turned to Dad. 'I am very sorry you have the anxiety of your other son's disappearance. I have no doubt he will turn up. Boys usually do. Meanwhile I must ask you to see that his brother here keeps his vivid imagination to himself. Ghost stories however ridiculous are not consistent with the image of the Abbey we are trying to promote. The Abbey is a pilgrim church. It is not some second-rate stately home that has to use ghost stories to attract business.'

Before Dad could say anything there was a knock at the door. The Dean's secretary entered. She said, 'I'm so sorry to interrupt you, Mr Dean, but it's the Press Association on the telephone. I've told them you are in a meeting and cannot be disturbed but they are threatening to send down a reporter if you do not make a statement.'

'A statement about what?' the Dean asked.

'They know Canon Ambrose is here,' she replied, 'and they know about young Jonny. They want to know whether there is any truth in the rumour that there might be a supernatural explanation for the boy's disappearance.'

Chapter 12

'There is no truth whatsoever!' boomed Mr Bullstrode so loudly he must have intended the Press Association to hear.

The Dean asked Dad when we could expect the copy of Major André's message

'By two at the latest.'

'Tell the Press Association I shall give them a statement at three. Before that I can make no comment.'

The meeting broke up. As he left, Mr Bullstrode warned that any suggestion to the press that Jonny's disappearance was connected with the all-night opening of the Abbey would be as good as throwing away a million pounds.

'I shall tell them as soon as possible,' the Dean assured him.

Canon Ambrose said that while they awaited further news he wished to check one or two things in the Abbey. Chief Inspector Dawkins left with him. Dad wanted me to go home to tell Mum that he would be staying at the Deanery until the message from Washington came through. But I had one more question up my sleeve.

I said to the Dean, 'I know you think I'm suffering from

shock or something, but I can remember Father Benedict saying you would know where he was buried.'

I cannot say he went pale at my question because he was pale enough already, but the way he glanced at the door to make sure Canon Ambrose and Inspector Dawkins had gone and then replied hesitantly, 'I know where Father Benedict is buried,' convinced me that there was more to it than that.

Dad must have thought so too because straightaway he asked whether Father Benedict's tomb was marked.

The Dean's answer was a strange one. He had never heard of Father Benedict until last month. The Abbey workmen had been digging in the South Aisle to clear a place for the last remains of Dame S--- T---, the famous actress, and had found a plain wooden coffin marked on the lid: 'Fr. Benedict.' They had called the Dean to ask what they should do and he had instructed them to move the monk's coffin a short distance to the west.

'Who else knows of this?' Dad asked.

'It was no secret,' replied the Dean, 'Shamus could have overheard someone talking about it.'

'But I didn't,' I protested.

I wasn't fussed. I knew things were going my way. Do you have days like that when one after another things turn out better than you dared to hope and you feel really high, and frightened too in case your luck doesn't last?

But mine did last. At half-past two the teleprinter copy of Major André's message came across the wire from Washington. Dad came running up the Deanery stairs so fast I knew the handwriting matched. I had been so sure, it was almost an anti-climax. Dad and the Dean were pretty shattered, but when Canon Ambrose returned he took the news calmly. The Dean asked his opinion.

'We must always look first for a natural and reasonable explanation,' the Canon replied.

'There isn't one,' said Dad.

'Not at the moment, I agree,' said the Canon, 'but that does not lead me to conclude that the message on that paper was written by a ghost.'

Dad wasn't satisfied with that. He pointed out that I could hardly have forged the handwriting of a man who had been executed in 1780.

'Believe me,' said Canon Ambrose, 'I share your bewilderment. But it is one thing to be bewildered and another to say that the dead can assume their earthly form and write notes on pieces of paper.'

'What if Father Benedict's crucifix is exactly as Shamus says it is?' Dad demanded.

That, the Canon readily agreed, would be a meaningful coincidence.

'A what?' I exclaimed.

He didn't answer me direct but said, 'Then we shall have to accept the possibility that you have been in communication with the other side.'

Dad sank back in his chair with a sigh. 'But will it bring us any closer to finding Jonny?' he asked.

Canon Ambrose did not answer but his silence said 'No.'

We moved to the study so that the Dean would be ready to take the telephone call from the press. I thought, was it really only this morning that I came to tell the Dean what had happened? Outside the window the spring sunshine had faded. It would be cold at night.

The telephone rang. To the reporter at the other end, the Dean made a brief statement: 'The Dean and Chapter are deeply concerned at the disappearance of one of the children in the Abbey family. They have informed the police and are co-operating with police enquiries. They have also informed Canon David Ambrose, the Church's spokesman on the supernatural, because they wish to assure themselves that every avenue is being explored.'

I could guess what the reporter said to that because the Dean told him firmly that there was no question of anyone seeing ghosts. The reporter was not satisfied but the Dean refused to say more. He replaced the receiver while the reporter was still talking.

'I'm afraid they're going to be difficult,' he commented.

He became so anxious about the press finding out that he had decided to open Father Benedict's tomb that I feared he might change his mind. But I shouldn't have worried. He was not the sort of person who went back on his word. He telephoned Mr Ridley, the caretaker, and gave the order for the tomb to be opened at eight o'clock which would be well clear of the Abbey's closing-time. I could imagine Mr Ridley's face. The Dean insisted on absolute secrecy: Mr Ridley must tell no one other than the two workmen needed to raise the stone.

'You'll have to tell Mr Bullstrode,' Dad said.

'Oh yes, I shall have to do that.' The Dean sounded weary at the thought.

Chapter 13

It was still light outside but in the Abbey the darkness, like an incoming tide, had already filled the corners and was spreading back across the floor. The Dean had ruled that the main lights should not be switched on. He feared that if the press were prowling around their suspicions would be aroused by lights shining long after the Abbey had closed. Oil lamps were carried by the two men from the Works Department, a rough-looking pair who made it clear that they did not like the job they had been given. The lamps were placed on the floor and lit by Mr Ridley who made a great show of turning down the wicks so that the flame was hardly visible. He gave instructions to the workmen and then stood over them as they began to scrape away the filling between the flag-stones.

Dad was standing with the Dean and Canon Ambrose right beside Sir Cloudesley Shovel's memorial. To my relief Mr Bullstrode had refused to attend.

Shovel's smooth, blank eyes looked over Dad's head at the workmen bending over their task. I wondered what he was thinking; and Major André too, so close by at the beginning of the nave. Father Benedict – I supposed – could hear the sounds above his head.

There's a low stone shelf against the wall near Shovel's memorial. Here I sat down. This was my moment of triumph. They would find the crucifix in the teeth of Father Benedict's skull. The all-night opening of the Abbey tomorrow would be cancelled. Thanks to my determination, Jonny would be set free. We might even be famous. Jonny would like that.

I leaned back and rested my head against the wall behind me. I looked up at the triforium on the other side of the choir. And saw Jonny.

He was just standing there, right at the edge, holding the side of one of the arches, a straight drop of sixty feet at his toes.

I wanted to shout to him to be careful but I couldn't give shape to the words. My mouth opened but the sound that came out was like a voice on a record-player that has slowed right down. I tried to force more speed into the words but my jaw was stiff.

The others hadn't noticed. I tried to stand up and move towards them but my legs were no better than my voice. I seemed to be under the influence of some drug that had spread a paralysis through my body. Yet I could see that Dad was talking to the Dean and Canon Ambrose and that the workmen were putting the stones on one side and taking up their pick-axes to break the hard surface of the earth. I could see them all but I couldn't reach them by movement or by sound.

Then, suddenly, I was released. I looked up at the triforium. Jonny had gone. He had probably decided to explore further. I looked for Dad and the others. They had gone too, taking their lamps with them. Unless I could find Jonny I would be alone in the Abbey, the one thing I had dreaded for as long as I could remember. I ran towards the High Altar thinking Jonny would have followed the line of the triforium in that direction.

I was right. There was someone standing in the section of the triforium above the North Porch. I could just see the white of his face in the darkness. But as I started towards him he fell. He dropped straight down and hit the chairs with a crash.

I jumped over the red rope that keeps the tourists away from the altar steps and ran to the spot where he had fallen. He was getting to his feet and brushing the dust off his sleeves. It wasn't Jonny. It was Lord Castlereagh. I recognised him at once. I was so relieved, I only just managed to say, 'Did you see Jonny up there?'

Lord Castlereagh was feeling his arms and legs.

'Not a bone broken,' he muttered with disgust.

I left him and hurried towards the West End of the Abbey. You reach the triforium by a door behind Lord Salisbury's tomb and a stone stair that winds up steeply to the bell-tower. The backs of your knees are aching before you reach the top.

Though it was dark on the stairs there was enough window-light at the top for me to see right along this section of the triforium. There was no sign of Jonny. I called to him but there was no reply. I walked as far as the right-angled turn where the triforium leaves the nave and follows the walls of the North Transept. From here I could see where Lord Castlereagh had been standing. There was no white face now in the shadows. I looked back across the top of the choir-stalls. The faint glow from the two oil lamps in the South Aisle just coloured the far wall. Dark shapes moved across the glow.

I went down to join them. As I approached Dad held out his hand and clasped mine.

'Excited?' he asked.

I nodded.

The two workmen were standing hip-deep in the hole they had made.

'Go easy now,' Mr Ridley told them.

It was the signal for us to move forward.

The workmen had cleared the earth from the coffin and were standing on either side of it, their boots white with dust. Mr Ridley turned up the flame in one of the lamps and held the lamp low over the tomb. The name 'Fr. Benedictus' was quite clear, deeply carved.

The Dean said a short prayer at which one of the workmen bowed his head and the other raised his eyes to heaven. Dad stared ahead of him.

The coffin lid groaned at the first upward pressure.

'Steady,' Mr Ridley warned.

After five hundred years the nails were hard to pull. Once they were free the lid came up easily. We all leaned forward to look inside.

I couldn't make it out at first. There just seemed to be a jumble of bones without shape. I couldn't see Father Benedict's crucifix and my stomach began to ache with anxiety that something had gone wrong.

'There are two people buried here,' said Canon Ambrose. 'Look, there are two skulls, one at that end and one at this.'

We stared at the bones, still unable to recognise a pattern.

54

It was Canon Ambrose who sorted it out for us. He pointed to the two spines, each leading away from its skull. The arms and legs were pretty mixed up but gradually I could make out the two skeletons. One skeleton was taller than the other.

Canon Ambrose noticed something else.

'This chap,' he said, kneeling at the edge of the tomb and tapping one of the skulls with his fingers, 'has a cracked skull and both his legs are broken. That's probably what killed him.'

'He's smaller too,' I said.

Canon Ambrose nodded. 'Hardly a full-grown man,' he agreed, 'but that wasn't unusual in those days.'

I felt a hand on my shoulder. It was the Dean. He said, 'Look there. The smaller one is holding a crucifix in his hand.'

He was right. The smaller figure was clutching the gold crucifix close to his ribs as though he was trying to hide it from his fellow skeleton.

That's typical Jonny, I thought. He's ruined everything.

Chapter 14

'You'll have to come to terms with it some time,' said Dr Rosewater.

'Do you think I'm going mad?' I asked him.

'I don't know. What do you think?'

That was typical of him. He kept turning my questions into questions of his own. He was the psychiatrist recommended by Dr Anderson. Mum had insisted that he should come round that evening even though it was well after nine when Dad and I returned from the Abbey. He was tied up at some clinic or other during the day anyway.

I liked him. He hadn't got a bedside manner and he didn't treat me like a child.

By way of replying to his question I said, 'I saw Jonny when we were in the Abbey this evening.'

'What did he say?'

'He didn't. He disappeared before I could catch up with him.'

I could hear Mum and Dad moving about quietly on the landing and talking in hushed voices as though someone had died.

'So what happens now?' he asked. He's always asking questions.

I shrugged.

'I'll have to tell the ghosts the deal's off.'

'They may not let Jonny go,' he warned.

I was prepared for that. I thought I could persuade the Grand Council to give me another chance. All they wanted was the Abbey to themselves between midnight and dawn. All I needed from them was better proof that they were not just people in my imagination. Father Benedict and Major André would think of something. The crucifix would have worked if Jonny hadn't been so dead set on boosting his savings bank account.

'What will convince them that the ghosts exist?' Dr Rosewater asked.

I looked at him sharply.

'You don't believe in the ghosts yourself,' I told him.

'No, but I'm interested in your solution to the problem.'

'There's only one thing people like Mr Bullstrode would understand,' I said, 'and that's if they met the ghosts themselves.'

'Can you arrange that?'

'I don't know. The ghosts would be taking a terrible risk. They might lose their chance of leaving the earth for ever.'

'Where do they go when they leave the earth?' he asked as though he was really interested.

'Father Benedict says it's just the next stage. Not heaven.'

'And if you can't persuade them to take the risk? You might have to come to terms with that, you know.'

I didn't answer. If he wanted to play games he could play them by himself. I had more important things to think about.

We sat in silence for a while and then he asked me how I was going to get in.

'In where?'

'Into the Abbey. You're going back again, aren't you?'

I told him.

'Sounds dangerous,' he commented, 'particularly if you're tired.'

He felt in his pocket and took out a small bottle of white pills. He unscrewed the top and shook two pills into his palm.

'Take these with a glass of water. They'll keep you wide-awake for twelve hours, then you'll go out like a light.'

I wasn't that stupid. So he lifted his hand and putting the palm across his mouth swallowed the pills himself.

'If they're sleeping pills,' he said, 'you'll see my eyelids dropping in five minutes.'

Big Ben began to strike ten. In two hours I would be with Jonny again. I was so eager for that moment, there was no chance of my feeling tired.

Dr Rosewater's eyelids showed no sign of dropping. He saw me watching him and smiled.

'Funny things twins,' he said, still holding the small bottle ready in case I changed my mind, 'there's a lot we don't know about them. Take you and Jonny. Who knows what you were cooking up before you were born. It seems you can communicate across time and space, even across death itself perhaps.'

'Jonny's not dead,' I snapped.

'No, but for the moment he's as good as, isn't he?'

I lost my temper. It just happens sometimes. I can't help it. When I do Dad says, 'Come on Shamus, grip,' which doesn't help much. Anyway he loses his temper sometimes too.

'He's *not* dead!' I shouted.

Dr Rosewater told me he would come back in the morning.

'Take care,' he added.

'I'm going mad, aren't I?' I said.

He had his hand on the door-handle.

'Possibly,' he replied as though madness was nothing to worry about, just a virus infection, 'but I don't think so.'

I didn't try to sleep. Mum and Dad did not even mention Dr Rosewater when they came in together to say goodnight.

Penelope popped her head round the door to ask: 'OK Shamus?'

'OK Penelope,' I replied.

At half-past eleven I pushed Dad's map-reading lamp into the pocket of my jeans and swung my legs through the open window. The lamp is small and flat, the sort of light a spy might use for checking papers. It doesn't shine very far but I thought it might come in useful. It was an easy drop on to the roof below. I walked along its flat stone edge to the fire escape and in two minutes I was in Dean's Yard.

I kept close to the wall. There were a number of cars parked with their front wheels against the curb. In one of them a man was sitting in the driver's seat, both hands together on the top of the steering-wheel and his head resting on his hands. Seeing him there nearly scared me out of the living daylights as I had not expected to see anyone. He might be ill or even dead. I approached and peered through the windscreen. It was Dr Rosewater and even with the windows closed I could hear his snoring. I laughed to myself. He had just managed to reach the car.

This encounter raised my spirits. It was a good omen. When, in the Abbey, the Dean had said there had been enough ghost-hunting and that now we must leave the search for Jonny in the hands of the police, I had hit one of my all-time lows. But outwitting Dr Rosewater gave me hope again.

I passed through the cloisters like one of the old ghosts, so silent, so swift. From the West Cloister I climbed out on to the moonlit lawn and walked to the bottom of the scaffolding that boxed in the Chapter House from top to toe. The Department of the Environment were repairing the medieval roof, had been for years now.

It was a wild climb even with the ladders the workmen had left. At any other time I would have refused point-blank to do it but now I hardly gave the risk a second thought. All the way up I was murmuring, 'You're crazy, Shamus, real crazy,' but I didn't believe it for a moment. It was just a joke I had with myself.

The route to the top was like finding your way through a vertical maze. I would reach one level of the scaffolding and then have to hunt round for the next ladder which might be on the other side of the building. At some levels there were planks tied to the scaffolding so that it was easy to move horizontally but at others I had to swing along the pipe like a monkey.

There was still traffic coming and going along the Embankment but there was little chance of my being spotted. The scaffolding had a corrugated iron roof to keep the rain out of the Chapter House and for most of the climb I was in its shadow.

At the level below the corrugated iron I climbed off the scaffolding on to the stone battlements from which the Abbey roof rose steeply into the night sky.

Between the battlement and the roof was a broad gutter. Here I sat down to rest. Even at this late hour the glow of the city coloured the night sky so that the clouds seemed to reflect a great fire. I breathed deeply and gazed out over the roofs of London. The most dangerous part of my climb was surely behind me.

It was easy to move along the gutter to the dormer window in the Abbey roof. Jonny and I had often wondered what that window was for since it could not be seen from inside the Abbey. I knelt down and looked through the dusty glass. It was too dark to see anything clearly inside.

Have you ever tried to break a window? It was a lot harder than I had expected. I was not worried about the noise at this height and I was certain this remote window was not attached to the elaborate alarm system. But the glass wouldn't crack. I tried hitting it with the back of Dad's lamp and when that didn't work I sat back against the battlement and kicked the glass. My gym shoes did not make good hammers but at the fourth kick the glass cracked. From then it was easy. I opened a hole by picking out the loose triangles of glass and put my hand through to lift the catch.

The window was stiff but it opened. I switched on the lamp and leaned inside. There was a great timbered hall, so vast my light did not even reach the opposite wall, let alone the two ends. This attic under the roof must run the whole length of the Abbey. I lowered myself on to the stout cross-beams that made up the floor. I had no idea in which direction to go so I tried the right, probing the darkness as I moved from one cross-beam to the next. I tried to visualize what part of the Abbey was beneath and reckoned that I was over the choir and approaching the point where the two transepts joined the main aisle to the High Altar.

My torch picked out a door about two-thirds normal size. It was set in a wooden wall that stretched the full width of the roof. Perhaps this was the way down to the triforium. The door was bolted on my side but there was no lock.

The bolt moved easily but the door, instead of opening towards me as I had expected, swung away as the bolt was clear. This unexpected movement caught me off balance. My hand was still on the bolt and I allowed the door to draw me forward. To my horror I saw that there was nothing beyond but space. The door led nowhere. In front of me was the emptiness of the Abbey and a straight drop to the chequered paving below.

I would have fallen if my left hand had not been gripping the door-frame. As it was, my right arm and shoulder swung out into space as I released the door. It was only a fraction of a second but in that time I was tempted to let go as though it wouldn't have mattered because I could have picked myself up off the floor like Lord Castlereagh.

Then the shock hit me and I drew back shuddering.

'Christmas!' I exclaimed aloud. I collapsed on to the beams and held my arms across my chest to stop the shivering. I heard Big Ben strike midnight but only faintly.

It must have been several minutes before I had the nerve to go forward again for when I looked down the ghosts were already there.

_____Chapter 15_____

I thought of shouting but decided against it. After the shock I was half afraid that it was risky even to let words fall all that way. I went back along the roof in the hope of finding a way down to the triforium. Dad's lamp seemed hardly more than a pinprick in this vast cavern of darkness.

At last I reached what I assumed to be the West End of

the Abbey. The roof pitched down and there was a door to my right. This time I took no chances. I approached the door as gingerly as though I expected it to be booby-trapped. It was unlocked. I opened it a little and saw a flight of broad wooden steps leading down to the level of the triforium. It was empty but I could see through the triforium arches that the nave was crowded.

The key was on the other side of the door. Before going down I took it out and placed it in the lock on the roof side. If I had to make a quick escape I could lock the door behind me and have time to climb through the window before the door was broken down.

From the triforium I looked at the mass of ghosts in the nave. It seemed incredible that anyone in his right mind could doubt that all these people existed. I couldn't see Jonny but he was probably up at the East End with Father Benedict and the others.

I went down the winding stone stair to the ground level and waited for a while in the shadow of Lord Salisbury's tomb. I could sense the excitement and the anticipation in the crowd. The thought that it was my arrival they were awaiting and my answer on which they pinned their hopes sent a fizz through me. I had not brought good news. Perhaps they would read that in my face and tear me limb from limb before I had a chance to explain to Father Benedict.

'Grip, Shamus, grip!'

I emerged and walked as confidently as I dared into the crush. They made no attempt to stop or talk to me. But heavens, they smelt awful! What had seemed at a distance a sweet smell of pinewoods and summer dust, was sickening close to. The smell was so strong, so rich with decay, it was like breathing in death itself. I pressed my lips together in case I took a fatal dose.

The ghosts were so closely packed I could not avoid

touching them as I pushed my way through. I hated that touch. The combination of sickly smell and ice-cold skin made my head dizzy with disgust.

I tried not to look up at their faces but thrust forward as quickly as I could and as roughly as I dared with my head down. I thought, they must hate me for being young and alive. As the crowd began to thin I raised my head and saw I was almost at the choir-screen. With a feeling of relief, I broke into a run. Almost at once my legs hit a child or dwarf and I stumbled and fell. I should have got up quickly and pressed on but I turned to see who I had stumbled over. It was neither a child nor a dwarf. It was the man I had seen from the organ loft the previous night, the soldier who had been shot in half by a canonball and who carried his legs on his back. He was rocking on his hips like one of those dolls on round bases that you can hit as hard as you like but never knock over.

I was so turned off by the sight of him I could not say anything. I tried to get to my feet but the crowd had closed in. Their frozen hands started to beat softly on my head and shoulders. I didn't know whether they were hitting me in anger or touching me out of curiosity, but I didn't propose to wait and find out. I forced my way up and barged into the mob in the direction of the screen. It wasn't difficult to push through but I hated the sensation. It was like running into a forest of dead trees: the branches bent and snapped or thrust sharp fingers at your face.

I cleared the worst and ran under the organ loft into the choir. The ghosts in the choir-stalls watched me pass without much interest. There was still no sign of Jonny but as I sprang up the altar steps I heard his voice cry, 'Hey Shamus!'

It sounded close by but I could not see him. 'Where the hell are you?' I shouted, angry because the ghosts had frightened me.

'Here,' the voice replied.

It came from behind the altar so I opened the door that led behind the altar screen to the Shrine of St Edward and the Royal Tombs.

Jonny was sitting on the flat top of Edward Longshanks' tomb, swinging his legs and laughing, though heaven knows what there was to laugh at. Father Benedict and the other members of the Grand Council were sitting or standing among the Royal Tombs. Looking from face to face I saw the same tense anticipation I had sensed among the ghosts in the nave. I also saw a stranger. He was a knight in full armour including a helmet with a single narrow slit for the eyes. That dark slit in which no eyes were visible gave me the spooks.

The ghosts were looking at me and must have read failure in my expression.

'They did not believe you,' said Father Benedict quietly.

I shook my head.

'It was Jonny's fault,' I said.

'It was not!' Jonny exclaimed.

'Yes it was. You had the crucifix in your hand.'

'But my message,' Major André cut in, 'did not that persuade them?'

I said, 'It was right, every word of it. Even the handwriting. But it wasn't enough. They just don't believe in ghosts.'

There was a silence that seemed to be full of despair. Henry of Lancaster stepped forward. The knight, I notice, moved forward too as though he was Henry's man.

'I told you, Father, I told you all,' said Henry, obviously determined to take command of the situation. 'It was foolish to try to bargain with these people. They have sold their souls for money. They are not in a position to compromise. If we want the Abbey for ourselves we must fight for it.'

He looked all round to see who would dare defy him.

Admiral Shovel was not impressed. 'This is not the field of Agincourt, Lancaster, and we are not your captains,' he said slowly, 'nor will the enemy be impressed by the sharpness of your steel.'

'O brave Shovel,' Henry sneered. 'Do you know how he died?' he asked the rest of us. 'A fisherman's wife found him washed up on the beach and smothered him with her skirts for the ring on his finger. A hero's death, Admiral! I do not wonder that fighting is not much to your taste.'

Shovel rode the attack like an experienced boxer riding a flurry of blows. You knew they had not hurt him. Calmly, he told Father Benedict that in his opinion violence was not the way.

'But my dear Shovel, we have nothing else to offer,' said Mr Fox.

'We have the boy.' said Lancaster. 'This time we send an ultimatum. Either the Abbey is ours between midnight and dawn or they will never see this child again.'

I glanced at Jonny. I think he was more put out at being called a child than frightened by what Henry was proposing. That's the trouble with Jonny. He doesn't even take danger seriously, but I began to think of ways in which we could escape.

For some time the argument raged in the Grand Council. The ghosts divided as before. Henry of Lancaster, Mr Fox and Lord Francis Villiers were for a direct confrontation, using violence if necessary to force the living souls to recognize their ghosts' existence. Their argument was that Jonny was no use as a hostage until the living souls accepted that it was the dead souls with whom they had to deal. Major André, Ben Jonson and Admiral Shovel were in favour of one last attempt to convince the living souls without a direct confrontation which carried with it the risk of eternal punishment. The knight did not vote or speak.

He lurked at Henry's shoulder, silent and sinister.

Father Benedict did not intervene. He let the argument burn itself out. Sometimes it flared up again when you thought it was dead.

Henry dominated the discussion. He didn't bluster. His cold, strong voice cut like the sharp sword he wished to use. He dismissed his opponents as 'a sailor who lost his fleet, a spy hanged as a pick-pocket and a common scribbler'. He accused them of cowardice, he told them they were more interested in their own promotion than in freedom for all the ghosts.

I could hear the argument going his way. What made it worse was that I half agreed with him. I could see no point in violence but unless people like Mr Bullstrode were forced to confront a dead soul they would never believe. This much I told Father Benedict when at last he turned to me. He nodded and looked round the group to see that the discussion had finished. No one spoke. They awaited his judgment.

'I believe Shamus is right,' he said, 'the living souls will not believe unless they can encounter someone from our side. But let it be one who has less to lose by the postponement of his case. He will confront the living souls at their official opening of the Abbey tonight. Then they will believe and agree to our terms for the boy's release.'

'We shall be blamed,' said Shovel, 'whoever confronts them, we shall be blamed.'

'Sweet Saviour!' Henry exclaimed. 'Whatever possessed them to give you a command?'

'I earned it,' Shovel replied as steady as ever. 'Unlike you I was not born to command.'

'That,' said Henry, 'is the truest word you have spoken.'

Father Benedict ignored them as though they were squabbling children.

I asked what I should tell the Dean.

'Tell him that we shall give him proof he cannot gainsay,' he replied. 'Do not tell him how but tell him when. We shall need a written agreement, signed by both sides. His lawyers can draw up the document; you know the terms. I shall meet him myself for the signing at midnight tomorrow night at the Great West Door.'

'That will be the end of us all,' said Shovel mournfully.

'We have no choice,' Father Benedict told him.

Chapter 16

'I don't mind really,' said Jonny, 'I quite like being dead.'

I was furious with him. It was so typical. He liked being with kings and famous men; and he didn't object to sleeping all day.

'You've got to come back,' I told him, 'think of Mum and Dad.'

'They can come and visit me,' he replied as if a grave was a hospital bed.

'What about your football?' If that didn't touch him nothing would.

He said, 'There are quite a lot of boys here. They're not bad. And there's a horse. That knight who was here was buried with his horse.'

'Oh for God's sake be serious, Jonny,' I said.

I was worried. If he did not have the will to come back, it made my job ten times harder.

The members of the Grand Council had gone to explain to the other ghosts what was planned. I could not tell from the rise and fall of the crowd's response how well the plan was being received.

67

Jonny jumped down from the tomb on which he was sitting.

'Hey Shamus, I'll show you the horse.'

I grabbed his arm. 'Jonny, you've got to come back.'

'OK I will. What are you worried about?' he asked, brushing past me and making off in the direction of Henry VII's chapel.

He was right about the horse. It was a magnificent animal, huge and strong like a brewer's dray-horse with two white patches on its rich black coat. Where on earth had they found room to bury it? It stood proud and still, hardly aware of the ghosts now streaming round the Ambulatory as they came away from the meeting. Occasionally it lifted one of its front feet and struck the stone floor with a great iron horseshoe.

The knight who had lurked at Hentry's shoulder was tightening one of the saddle-straps. I asked Jonny who he was.

'Sir Lewis Somebody-or-Other,' he told me, 'he fought with Henry at Agincourt. Major André says he's round the twist.'

'Why?'

'How should I know. Someone probably hit him on the head.'

'He ought to see Dr Rosewater,' I said.

The knight turned his head as we approached. Even close to I could not catch any glimpse of eyes in the darkness of his helmet. The nasty thought occurred to me that there might not be any eyes to see. He didn't speak. When Jonny asked if we could have a ride, he answered with a brief movement of his helmet.

It was the devil of a job getting on to the horse. The knight gave us no help. Eventually we found that by climbing up the side of Sir Lewis's own memorial we were in a position to jump on to the horse's back. The horse didn't budge.

We might have been sparrows landing for all it noticed.

Sir Lewis took the rein and led the horse out towards the North Transept. Was this what he did each night to pass the time? A bit of a come-down after Agincourt, I thought. Perhaps it was this that had driven him out of his mind.

Ghosts looked up as we passed. I sensed from their expressions that Father Benedict had put the plan across successfully. The tension and hostility had gone. One or two ghosts even raised their hands in greeting and smiled with a mouthful of rotting black teeth. In the nave we were given a cheer. Jonny waved. You would have thought he had won the Cup single-handed.

The night passed. It was good to be with Jonny again, though I felt a bit out of it at times because he knew all the younger ghosts and I didn't. I might have known he would soon make friends with the princes murdered in the Tower. They joined us on the horse for a while and then the four of us went off to do some climbing. I had never realized what marvellous climbs there were in the Abbey. Dad takes us down to Kent sometimes to climb on Harrison's Rocks but they're not a patch on some of the Abbey memorials. One of the best climbs is up the south side of Poets' Corner to the steps that lead to the old monks' dormitory. You can climb the whole way on the Duke of Argyll's monument but the last part is tricky because you have to balance on his head with one foot while you swing the other up on to the stairs. The princes were better climbers than we were but, as Jonny told them, they'd had a lot longer to practise.

I liked Prince Edward the better. He was quieter than Richard who was always laughing at Jonny's bad jokes. Edward introduced me to his mother, Elizabeth Woodville. He hadn't seen her for five hundred years; then one night a few years ago she appeared with the rest of the ghosts at midnight. You can imagine how he felt. Some workmen on a building site in Stepney had found her coffin and the

Dean had allowed her to be reburied in the Abbey.

The sky outside the Abbey windows began to pale. Most of the ghosts had gone back to their tombs by now. Jonny and I were sitting on the altar with the princes when Father Benedict came up and sat with us for a while.

I really liked him. I can't explain exactly what it was that was different about him; he had this strength that you couldn't see but you knew was there. I don't mean he'd win in a fight, not that sort of strength. You felt he could have all the bad luck in the world and still not complain, still not give in. It was as if he had strength stored inside him like you store electricity and when he needed it he drew out just enough to see him through. I'd never met anyone like him before.

We had been silent for a time, each of us busy I suppose with his own thoughts and hopes for the coming day, when Father Benedict said quietly, 'I love this hour. Each morning a bell woke us for matins. One of our brothers came ahead to light the candles so that even in mid-winter the Abbey always welcomed us.' He put his hand on my shoulder. 'You must love your brother,' he said.

'Love *him*!' I exclaimed. 'Not likely.'

Father Benedict laughed. 'Take care,' he said, 'God bless you.'

He looked up at the windows. It was time for them all to go. I think Jonny would have gone without saying goodbye, he was so absorbed with what he looked like in Richard's floppy velvet hat.

'See you Jonny,' I said as he wandered off, trying the hat this way and that.

'Hey Shamus, how do I look?' he called, pulling the hat down over one ear.

'A right nit,' I told him.

He laughed.

'See you Shamus.'

But I wondered whether I would ever see him again.

Chapter 17

Mr Bullstrode stood with one foot in the Dean's drawing-room and one in the corridor. He could not spare any more of himself to deal with this business.

'Any trouble, any trouble at all,' he growled at me, 'and you and your friends will be arrested. The police have their instructions.'

The Dean and Canon Ambrose sat with heads bowed waiting for the storm to pass.

'You can't arrest a ghost,' I pointed out.

'Anyone who tries to disrupt the official opening will be arrested,' Mr Bullstrode assured me, 'I don't care if it's the Devil himself.'

'I don't know who it'll be,' I said, knowing perfectly well it would annoy him.

He had already gone but hearing my remark he returned. He was one of those people who had to have the last word.

He said: 'It's not a psychiatrist you need, young man, it's a damn good hiding.'

He turned on his heel. I smiled to myself. He would eat his words soon enough.

The Dean raised his head. I had given him the ghost's message and he had called in Mr Bullstrode and Canon Ambrose at once.

Canon Ambrose eased himself further back in his armchair.

'Has it ever occurred to you, Edward,' he said, fixing his eyes on the ceiling, 'that Shamus may have had a unique experience, part subconscious, part supernatural? I don't mean we should accept what he says literally but that it is some sort of metaphor, an oblique, indirect communication from those who are buried in the Abbey.'

The Dean paused before answering. 'Even now I cannot believe that anything supernatural has occurred,' he said. 'Shamus is honest but the truth he is telling us is the truth of the imagination.'

'God can speak through the imagination,' Canon Ambrose reminded him, 'just as He can intervene in the natural order.'

'He can, He does intervene,' the Dean agreed, 'but it is always to some great purpose.'

Canon Ambrose put his fingertips together to make a church and rested one end against his lips as he spoke. 'Perhaps he does not wish His church to become a tourist attraction,' he said quietly.

The Dean sighed. 'You know that isn't fair, David. We have no grant from the Government. Without the money from tourism the fabric of the Abbey would rot. Then there would be no church.'

'There would be no building,' the Canon corrected him.

I let them talk. It was like listening to blind men when you can see.

The Dean stood up and walked to the window. He said: 'A boy is missing. His brother sees visions and dreams dreams. His parents are at their wits' end. The police have no clue. I cannot see the hand of God in that.'

Canon Ambrose rose too and went to stand beside him.

'You're a prisoner of common sense, Edward. Keep an open mind at least. If a ghost turns up at the official opening even Mr Bullstrode will have to come to terms with the supernatural.'

When I left the Deanery I did not go straight home. It was a bright but colder day with a sharp wind bending the dying daffodils in Canon Hildyard's window-boxes. I slipped across the Sanctuary to the line of telephone booths by the cab rank. I only had one ten p. piece so I had to make it tell.

I remembered that the journalist who had called the Dean had been from the Press Association. I looked up the number and dialled.

I thought the journalist might put the phone down and laugh away my ten-pence worth. But he didn't. He jumped at what I was saying as though this was just what he had been waiting for. I told who I was and what was going to happen at the official opening.

'Who will come from the other side?' he asked.

'I don't know. One of the Grand Council I expect. Perhaps Father Benedict himself.'

'That's just terrific!' he exclaimed. 'You'd better get there early. Every damned journalist in the country will be there.'

Dr Rosewater was talking to Mum in the kitchen. I kissed Mum and she put her arm round me. She was warm.

Dr Rosewater said, 'I hope you slept well.'

I smiled. He was a good loser. He was sitting on the side of the kitchen table swinging a leg. When Mum had gone he asked whether I had seen Jonny last night. I told him that I had.

'He doesn't blame you, does he?' he asked.

I shook my head. Jonny was enjoying himself. There was nothing to blame anyone for.

'Isn't it time you stopped blaming yourself?'

'I could have stopped him,' I replied.

'But it was his idea. He knew the risks.'

I said nothing. I didn't think Jonny ever thought about risks. He was one of those people who didn't have to. When he ran races he came first. When he kicked the ball it went into the corner of the net. He was a winner. I suppose he thought he always would be. If he went to war the bullets would miss him and if he slipped on a mountain the rope would hold. Dad says there's no such thing as luck. But I don't agree. Jonny was born lucky.

I remembered what it was I wanted to tell Dr Rosewater. Jonny liked being a ghost; he wasn't all that keen to come back.

I saw the light come on in Dr Rosewater's eyes even though he turned his head away to hide it. He asked, 'Could you ever accept that if you knew that he was happy?'

I shook my head. I would never accept that. Jonny would soon get bored with the ghosts anyway. He always gets bored easily.

If Dr Rosewater was disappointed with that answer he didn't show it. Instead he asked me about the official opening that evening. I told him that one of the ghosts was going to appear.

'It should be an interesting occasion,' he said, though I knew perfectly well that he didn't believe a word I said.

Chapter 18

I had expected a bigger crowd. There were the coach parties of tourists who wanted to be the first to see the Abbey at night. There were the representatives of the City of Westminster and of those foreign countries that sent tourists to Britain. And there were the press, mostly cameramen with their gear hanging heavily at their sides. If there were policemen, as Mr Bullstrode had warned, they must have been in plain clothes.

The chairs had been cleared from the nave to enable all who wish to attend the ceremony to do so under cover. The bright, cold day had turned to drizzle in the early evening. Standing about halfway up the nave and facing the crowd was the official party: the Dean, the Lord Mayor, the Chairman of the Tourist Board and Mr Bullstrode. In front of them was a microphone on a stand and at one side two men and a woman who turned out to be interpreters.

Above us the chandeliers sparked but the East End of the Abbey was still in darkness. Abbey stewards in tail-coats restrained the crowd with small gestures of the hand.

The ceremony dragged. For the sake of the tourists each speech was translated into French, German and Japanese. The Lord Mayor spoke briefly. The Dean welcomed and blessed the pilgrims from many lands. The Chairman of the Tourist Board mentioned the sum of money earned by tourism in the previous year. Now Mr Bullstrode was speaking and by my watch he had already taken eight and a half minutes.

I was standing in the front row with Dad and Canon Ambrose. Behind us the tourists were becoming restless. A steward, turning his face to them, put a finger to his lips and raised his eyebrows.

I was excited and happy inside myself. I alone knew that everything would turn out all right. I could not believe the Dean and the Chapter would refuse the ghosts' terms once they had been confronted by a man from the other side of death. I kept looking at the choir-screen wondering whether it would be Father Benedict himself who would appear out of the darkness.

Mr Bullstrode droned on. He was explaining that tourism helped people from different countries to understand one another but few seemed to be listening. The crowd was anxious to get on with the business of exploring the Abbey.

At last Mr Bullstrode finished. The loud applause was an expression of relief.

But then the translations began. The crowd grew restless and the stewards walked along the front row like policemen at a football match.

It was during the final Japanese translation of Mr

Bullstrode's speech that I heard the faint but familiar clicking sound and tried to remember what it was. If Mr Bullstrode was boring in English, he was unbearable in Japanese. The clicking continued and now others could hear it too. It was a hard, metallic sound. Then I remembered. It was the horse. Its hooves were clipping the stone floor in the Ambulatory.

So Father Benedict had sent the horse. The one who had least to lose by the postponement of his case – it was the perfect answer.

Should I run forward now or wait until the horse appeared? The metallic clip-clopping was so loud, so unmistakable, members of the official party were glancing over their shoulders. Mr Bullstrode whispered something in the Dean's ear and they both looked in my direction. The Japanese interpreter struggled on though he had completely lost the attention of his audience.

I think I actually muttered to myself, 'Go, Shamus, go!' I slipped out of Dad's hand resting on my shoulder and dashed forward. A steward tried to grab me but I twisted easily out of his grasp.

'He's coming!' I shouted. 'Listen, he's coming!'

'Arrest that boy!' cried Mr Bullstrode.

But he was too late. I had burst through the gap between the official party and the interpreters and was running towards the choir.

Then I stopped. The great, black horse was coming through the choir-stalls. But not only the horse. On its back was the knight. I recognized the armour and the narrow slit across the face of the helmet. Sir Lewis was carrying a lance which he lowered to the horizontal as he passed under the screen. He looked ready for battle.

Just this side of the screen, horse and rider halted. As they did so the tourists began to applaud. They thought Sir Lewis was part of the ceremony and the fact that he arrived early while the Japanese interpreter was still at work increased their enthusiasm. Clearly, the knight was a sort of visual aid provided by the Tourist Board. Even the official party was joining reluctantly in the applause though I could see the expressions of anger and bewilderment on their faces. The press men had broken ranks and were running forward to take close-up pictures.

As the applause died down the Chairman of the Tourist Board walked towards me smiling stiffly to show what a good sport he was. Behind him a uniformed police officer had materialized at last and was approaching the official party for instructions.

'Arrest that horseman,' I heard Mr Bullstrode say, though he tried to keep his voice down to deceive the crowd.

I looked up at Sir Lewis. Both he and his horse were quite still.

Flash-bulbs blazed suddenly all around them. The policeman advanced. I should have warned him that Sir Lewis was not an ordinary ghost but an insane one.

Sir Lewis held his lance tight against his side, the point steady an arm's length beyond the horse's head. Then he hunched his shoulders, tucked his iron chin on to his chest and pressed his spurs just once into the horse's flanks.

The horse moved forward so deliberately it might have been caught by a slow motion camera. But that movement was deceptive. Within a few seconds the horse was thundering down the nave, its great hooves battering the flag-stones.

The policeman leapt to one side leaving the official party exposed. The Dean appeared to raise a hand as if to say, 'Let us discuss this like reasonable men,' but he was swept aside, falling against Mr Bullstrode who lost his balance too and staggered back into the arms of the Japanese interpreter.

The crowd hesitated. Was this part of the act, the

77

horseman charging and drawing up miraculously at the very feet of the spectators? Or had something gone badly wrong, the horse, even the horseman, crazed by the flashing bulbs?

That hesitation was disastrous. When they realized that the horse was not going to stop, it was too late to get out of the way. With screams such as the Abbey had surely never heard before, men and women tore at one another to escape from the horse's path and from the point of the lance.

The horse hit the struggling mass and seemed to go straight through it as easily as if the crowd was tall grass or a field of corn. God knows how many people were trampled under the horse's hooves. I could not believe that this was what Father Benedict had intended but then I remembered that Sir Lewis was Henry's man.

At the West Door Sir Lewis made a tight turn and started back the way he had come. Desperate efforts were made to pull the injured out of his path. But most of the tourists and other guests were too busy scrambling to safety themselves to worry about those lying on the floor. They climbed on to monuments, using their feet to kick away those who tried to share their refuge. They tried to climb the pillars but could not find a foothold. They ran this way and that like frightened animals. They made strange cries.

All this time I stood quite still. There was nothing I could do. I prayed that no one had been badly hurt. Violence had not been necessary. But never again could anyone say that I was shocked or mad or living in my imagination. The ghosts had encountered the living souls with a vengeance.

Chapter 19

As Sir Lewis passed me on his way back to the choir, I thought I caught a brief nod of his helmet. Then he rode under the screen and into the darkness.

Someone cried, 'Lock the gates!' And another, 'Lock all the gates, we've got the bastard trapped.'

'What about the East Cloister Door?'

'It's locked already.'

How brave they had become. A hundred men, it seemed, were prepared to take command.

I suppose I should have realized that their fear would turn to anger and that some of their anger would be turned against me. I didn't even have a chance to defend myself. Men and women rushed at me striking at my head and shoulders with their fists and the flat of their hands. I put up my arms to shield my head and crouched low to take the force out of their blows. But then they started kicking me and that really hurt. They called me 'Traitor' and 'Ghost-lover', and one of them spat at me.

Somewhere beyond the battle I heard Dad shouting, 'Leave my son alone,' and I shouted back, 'Dad, help me.' At least he hadn't said, 'Grip, Shamus, grip.'

It was the police who rescued me. They had arrived in force from Cannon Row and Rochester Row. Dad held me in his arms to protect me from the last wild swipes but I told him, 'Not too tight.' The bruises were beginning to ache. It took the police half an hour to clear the Abbey and until they had, no attempt was made to pursue Sir Lewis. Ambulances took the injured to St Thomas' Hospital, the whine of the sirens continuing almost non-stop. Chief Inspector Dawkins said it was a miracle no one had been killed though a dozen had been seriously injured.

A St John's Ambulance man put some ointment on the

worst of my bruises. It was only then that I noticed that Dad, too, had been hit. There was a dark stain under his left eye.

Mr Bullstrode wanted to have me arrested there and then but Inspector Dawkins told him firmly that this was now a matter for the police and they would decide whether anyone was to be arrested.

'Who was the horseman?' Inspector Dawkins wanted to know.

I told him. He was Sir Lewis, a knight who had fought at Agincourt and was buried in the Abbey.

Dad said: 'Shamus, no more of that. Not now. We must know the truth. No one's blaming you for what happened but the police must know who that man was. Where did you meet him?'

'It *is* the truth, Dad. When they go in there they won't find him. He's been dead for five hundred years.'

Inspector Dawkins shook his head. He took Dad to one side. I bet he was saying, 'You ought to get a good psychiatrist to see that boy.'

He raised his voice to give his orders. The police marksmen were to stand by while unarmed officers made a search. He did not want any shooting unless it was absolutely necessary. The gates of the choir were opened and about thirty unarmed officers went through.

The Abbey was quiet. The Dean and Mr Bullstrode spoke in whispers. Neither had been hurt but both looked pretty shaken. Canon Ambrose stood apart, watching me.

The police marksmen waited, the brown-handled revolvers in leather holsters looking awkward and out of place against the dark blue uniform. From beyond the screen there was the occasional sound of voices as instructions were given and acknowledged. I did not expect anything else.

When the policemen returned they reported that they

had found no trace of the rider or the horse. Inspector Dawkins asked if they had checked every possible area. They assured him that they had. What was more, they had found that the East Cloister Door and the North Door were locked and bolted on the inside. There was no way any living person could have escaped let alone a horse.

They all fought against the truth even then. I could almost feel them searching for some other explanation.

The Dean asked Canon Ambrose what he thought.

'What can I think?' replied the Church's authority on the supernatural, 'I just don't understand. That's the honest answer. None of us does. Except Shamus perhaps. If we accept what he has been telling us all along, we have got to throw away all our existing ideas about life after death.'

'But is it possible that the horseman was dead, had been dead for centuries?' asked the Dean.

Canon Ambrose replied slowly and deliberately, 'We must now accept that possibility.'

'I suppose there is a Sir Lewis buried here,' said Inspector Dawkins, sticking to facts.

'Oh yes that is true,' the Dean replied. 'Sir Lewis Robessart. He was Henry the Fifth's Standard Bearer. He's buried in the South Ambulatory with his horse. The horse was Henry's idea; it fought well at Agincourt.'

He turned to Mr Bullstrode.

'We shall have to close the Abbey until this is all sorted out.'

Bullstrode shook his head.

'There must be some other way,' he said but his voice had lost all its old confidence. It had shrunk; it was half the voice it had been.

Without batting an eyelid I said: 'The ghosts will be expecting to meet you at midnight tomorrow to sign the agreement.'

They all looked at me. I do not know exactly what it was I

read in their expressions but I do know that it wasn't pity or contempt. Even Inspector Dawkins was studying me with his blue eyes as though I was a piece of evidence he now realized he would have to consider seriously.

A police sergeant came up to say that a large number of press men were waiting at the West Door. They refused to leave until they had a statement from the Dean or the officer in charge of the case. In a few hours, I thought, the truth about the ghosts will be broadcast all over the world.

_____*Chapter 20*_____

How shall I describe the next twenty-four hours? They were the most fantastic of my life – so far that is. I suppose I must have slept that night but all I can remember is lying awake in the early hours thinking, 'This time tomorrow Jonny will be home.'

In the morning there was a police guard on our house and other policemen were patrolling the Abbey precincts. The reason was soon clear. Thousands of sightseers were converging on Westminster. They had heard about the ghostly horseman on the news bulletins. I had become famous overnight. Penelope went out and bought all the morning papers. There were crowds already, she said, hundreds of people walking down Victoria Street towards the Abbey.

The headlines in the papers were so big you could have read them a long way away. Some of them had Jonny's name in them. That's typical Jonny. He was famous without lifting a finger. 'Is Jonny a hostage of the dead?' one headline asked. All the papers but one took it for granted that the ghosts would appear at midnight to sign the agreement and hand over Jonny. The exception was Dad's paper, *The Times*. It was so cautious it was pathetic; all the headlines said was 'Unusual Incident at Abbey Opening. Horse and rider evade police.' But I didn't think many people would take any notice of that and I was right. All through the morning the crowds kept coming. Over the radio the police appealed to people to stay at home. But the pull of the ghosts was too strong. Soon all the approaches to the Abbey were blocked and traffic had to be diverted. By mid-afternoon even the diversions were blocked. People just wanted to be sure to be near the Abbey when midnight came even if they could not see what was happening.

The Dean had announced that he was willing to meet the representatives of the ghosts. He denied charges that he was giving in to blackmail. The Dean and Chapter had reconsidered their decision to open the Abbey all night and had come to the conclusion that the building needed 'a period of rest' between midnight and dawn. He would be signing an agreement to this effect with the representatives of the ghosts but only on the condition that young Jonathan was restored to his family. In answer to a question, he had agreed that it would be the first time in the history of the world that the living and the dead had met officially.

That wasn't all. Mr Bullstrode had quite recovered his confidence. He had had an inspiration. If the ghosts really did appear at midnight and were seen on television in every country, the Abbey would become the most important pilgrim shrine in the world. It would increase its revenue many times over. It would no longer matter that by holding Jonny hostage the ghosts had forced the Abbey authorities to abandon their plans for an all-night opening. The large entrance fee that it would now be possible to charge at the Great West Door would more than compensate.

'There's no end to the promotional possibilities,' Mr Bullstrode told Dad. He was bubbling over with ideas for exclusive photographs of the ghosts, for ghostly T-shirts and lapel badges; he had even considered opening a number of tombs and selling off the bones at a high price as 'pieces of true ghost'.

He had come round to ask Dad's help with an idea for increasing the American market.

'Here's the young hero,' he boomed when he saw that I was in the room. You'd never have thought that he had wanted me arrested only a few hours before.

'We may need to set up a special company to handle it all,' he said.

'Ghosts Incorporated,' Dad suggested.

'Something like that,' said Mr Bullstrode, not noticing that Dad was laughing at him. 'I've been on to our lawyers. We can sell the television rights of tonight's show because it will take place on our property. I've told them to screw the maximum out of the television companies, particularly the foreign ones. They'll pay all right. It's like an outside broadcast of the resurrection. No one wants to be left out.'

'How much will you get?' Dad asked.

'Enough to clean the North Face three times over,' was Mr Bullstrode's triumphant reply.

I thought of the ghosts. What would they make of all this razzmatazz?

'They might be frightened by the crowds,' I warned.

Mr Bullstrode steadied his eyes on me as though trying to get me into focus.

'Who, the ghosts? Don't worry, they'll come. They need an agreement just as much as you need your brother back.'

'Even so,' said Dad, 'if Shamus has got it right about this Promotion Board of theirs, they'll want to keep the encounter with living souls as short as possible.'

'That's where Major André comes in,' said Mr Bullstrode. 'We can't have these ghost fellows nipping back into the Abbey when the whole world wants to get a look at them.

We need a second part of the ceremony and I've just the thing. You know the American Ambassador. I want you to ask him to be here at midnight to present Major André with a free pardon.'

'A bit late for that, isn't it?' Dad chuckled.

He was happy now Jonny would soon be safely home. But Mr Bullstrode was serious.

'Certainly not. It's not as if he can't remember. Think what it'll mean to him after all this time. And it will capture the imagination of the Americans. That's the point. Now if you could telephone the Ambassador ...'

'He just wanted to be shot,' I told him, 'that's all.'

'Perhaps we could arrange a firing squad,' said Dad cheerfully.

But Mr Bullstrode would not be put off.

I left them and went upstairs to see what Mum was doing. She was making a 'Welcome Home' cake for Jonny.

'Are you going to be there, Mum?' I asked her.

'No, darling, I'll stay and make sure everything's ready here. Jonny won't have had anything to eat for a long time.'

That's unlike Jonny, I thought.

The mild spring day faded slowly to dusk. I was so excited I couldn't settle down to anything. It was like Christmas only more so. I wasn't allowed outside even though the whole Abbey precincts had now been sealed off by police. I couldn't rest though Mum said I ought to try. I watched the television broadcasts from outside the Abbey but they only made me more nervous. There were bright lights everywhere and tightly-packed crowds. All the windows were dark with figures and there were people standing on the roofs of the buildings. The television commentator said that hundreds of thousands of people were still pouring into London so that they could say that they had been in the city at the very moment when the dead came back to the living.

85

'Why, Dad?' I asked.

Mr Bullstrode had left and we were sitting together in front of the television. Dad didn't answer immediately. He just sat listening to the commentary. At last he said: 'Because it's never happened before.'

While Dad was talking, one of the commentators was trying to work out how many people would be watching the broadcast at midnight. I thought I heard him say, 'One thousand million, that is a quarter of the world's population.'

'There've been stories of course,' Dad was saying, 'people who claimed to have seen ghosts, that sort of thing. But this is different. If the ghosts show up ...'

'They *will*,' I told him.

'Yes, I'm sure they will. Then it'll never be the same again. People won't be afraid of death any more. Not so afraid anyway.'

The commentator said that special flights were bringing visitors from the Continent and even from the United States. In New York a meeting of the United Nations General Assembly had been postponed so that the delegates could follow the events in London on television. A bishop appeared on the screen and was asked what these extraordinary events could mean.

'On the one hand they could be a sign from God,' he replied, 'but on the other hand they might be a trick of the Devil.'

'It'll never be the same again,' Dad repeated, and turning to smile at me added, 'Thanks to you, Shamus – Shamus the Famous.'

Mum wanted me to put on my school blazer and grey trousers but I told her that I ought to wear the same clothes I had worn in the Abbey so that the ghosts would recognize me straightaway.

'Well, I expect they will be looking their best,' she said, but Dad agreed with me so I kept my jeans and T-shirt on and pulled a sweater over the top in case the night was cold.

It was eleven-thirty. Half an hour to go. The Dean and his party would be calling for us any minute now. When the doorbell rang we said goodbye to Mum and Penelope and went downstairs. 'Good luck, Shamus,' Penelope called over the banister just as though I was going to play in a football match.

The Dean's party was small. Apart from the Dean himself there was only Canon Ambrose and Mr Bullstrode. The Dean was wearing a red cassock and a black gown. Canon Ambrose was all in black and Mr Bullstrode had on a tailed coat and striped trousers. Two policemen walked with us round the Yard to the gateway leading to the Sanctuary and Victoria Street. The men talked about the weather. I was amazed at the casualness of their conversation. It was unexpectedly quiet in Dean's Yard and the men spoke in soft voices, except when Canon Ambrose told a joke about Lazarus and then their laughter cracked like gunfire. I guessed they were just as nervous as I was, more so perhaps because at least I had met the ghosts before.

The huge iron gate under the archway was closed. As we neared it I heard the buzz of the crowd and the metallic sound of the walkie-talkies used by the police.

The Night Constable stood ready to open the small door in the gate.

'All right?' the Dean asked, looking at me.

I nodded.

One of the policemen said, 'Good luck, lad,' as the Night Constable unlocked the door and pulled it open. We followed the Dean through into the dazzling light of the television lamps. I couldn't see the crowds at first because my eyes were stunned by looking at the lamps, but I could hear the sound of their excitement rising and rising until it became a great roar. As we walked across the Sanctuary the people closest to us stretched out their hands. I didn't realize at first that it was me they wanted to touch.

The police had put crush barriers all around the Sanctuary but the crowds seemed to press in on us all the same. Some of the people at the barriers were kneeling. Others were cripples: they had come on crutches or been brought in wheel-chairs or on stretchers. The police had allowed the stretchers to be placed on the ground on our side of the barrier. Behind the cripples a man was holding a banner which said: 'Leave the dead alone.' As we passed I saw hands reach up from behind and pull the banner down.

'Stay close,' Dad said.

The Sanctuary is an open space in the shape of a triangle with the Great West Door of the Abbey on the shortest side. On one of the long sides are lawyers' offices; the other is open to Victoria Street. Mr Bullstrode had arranged for a temporary grandstand to be built in front of the offices so that the world's press would have a good view of the ceremony. They were on our right as we walked to the Abbey. On our left were the dense crowds. It was a fantastic sight. People seemed to be hanging all over the fronts of buildings like swarms of bees.

There were two television cameras on a scaffolding tower to the left of the Great West Door and a third on the ground in front of the press stand. In the centre of the Sanctuary a plain wooden table had been placed on the cobbles. Above it microphones were suspended on long rods like bait to catch every word of the ceremony. I could see one loudspeaker on the roof of the Abbey Bookshop and I guessed that there were many others in the surrounding streets.

As the roar of excitement that had greeted our arrival died away, a voice over the loudspeaker asked for silence for the Dean to say a few words. Dad and I stood with Canon Ambrose near the table. Mr Bullstrode busied himself with preparations, speaking to the television crews, checking points with Chief Inspector Dawkins and saluting members of the world's press as though they were his allies in a great enterprise.

Big Ben struck the third quarter.

The Dean started to speak:

'My friends, we have come together here not in our thousands but, thanks to the medium of television, in our millions. May I, on behalf of the Abbey, welcome you all, whatever your faith or uncertainty, whatever your race or nationality. As human beings we are bound by a common curiosity that is much stronger than all the forces that seek to divide us – a curiosity about the meaning of our lives and in particular about the meaning of our deaths. In a little under a quarter of an hour we may be wiser about the nature of death. But it would be wrong to pin all our hopes of eternal life on one encounter. It is not for us to understand all the mysteries of God's universe. So let us be quiet together for the remaining few minutes before midnight. Each of us will have his own thoughts. Some of us, I am sure, will be asking God's help in understanding the message of this night. Let us watch and pray in silence all over the world.'

The silence was complete. Even the television commentators were struck dumb. It was as though the world now emptied of all people and all animals. The breeze from the

89

river touched my cheek without a sound. I raised my eyes and glanced at the crowd. Dr Rosewater was standing in the front rank.

I went over to him.

'What are you doing here?' I asked.

He held out his right fist knuckles up. Then he turned the wrist full-circle and opened the fingers. In his palm were two small white pills.

'I should take them now,' he said, 'while there's still time.'

I laughed at him. 'You don't begin,' I told him, 'you don't begin to understand; you never will.'

_____*Chapter 22*_____

When Big Ben struck the hour the Dean turned to face the Great West Door. The crowd stirred but remained quiet. The voice of one of the commentators was just audible: 'This is the most astonishing moment in the history of the world.'

As the great clock laboured through the twelve strokes the Dean and Canon Ambrose crossed themselves quickly like athletes before an Olympic final. The last stroke rang away over the heads of the crowd. My heart thumped so loudly I was sure the microphones were picking it up. I stared at the Great West Door, straining my ears to catch the first hint of movement within.

The sound of the bolts being drawn back was unmistakable. One half of the door opened and then, without fuss or hesitation, three figures stepped out into the light. Somewhere far away in the heart of the vast crowd a voice was shouting hysterically like the cry of a wild bird.

Father Benedict came first, walking slowly but firmly

towards the table where the Dean was holding out both arms in welcome. Behind Father Benedict was Major André, holding his black hat against his right breast and walking proudly like the soldier he was. The third man was Henry of Lancaster. He looked proud too but also suspicious; more like a tiger than a soldier. He wore a red cloak and a heavy sword strapped to his side.

All three looked as alive as you or I except under the glare of the television lamps their skin looked pure white. They held their heads high; they were not ashamed of being dead. I thought they looked like warrior chieftains coming out to sign a treaty with the soldiers. They were undefeated and would sign as equals.

I was so proud of them and so thankful that they had kept their word that it did not occur to me to wonder why Jonny had not come out with them.

'Shamus!' Father Benedict saw me and held out his hand. I ran over to him and he put his arms round me.

That broke the crowd's silence. They cheered so loudly you could have heard them far away. They cheered and whistled and clapped. I turned to face them. The men and women nearest me were laughing and crying at the same time. One of the camera crew was just standing there with tears pouring down his face and shaking his head as though he still couldn't believe what he was seeing.

I took Father Benedict's cold hand and led him to the Dean. I don't think the Dean was sure whether to embrace the dead monk or shake his hand; I left them to sort that out while I greeted Major André. He bent down to whisper in my ear: 'We've go to be quick. The Promotions Board are furious about the whole business. Lancaster is threatening to cut down anyone who tries to delay us.'

The Dean was introducing Father Benedict to the crowd. I suspected that Henry was already impatient with such formalities. I said hallo to him.

We hadn't liked one another from the start. He gave me his most haughty look.

'Is Jonny OK?' I asked, embarrassed that he wouldn't even say hallo.

At the mention of Jonny's name Henry's face seemed to relax. He didn't smile but I reckon he came as close to it as he ever had before in life or in death. That's typical Jonny. He has this charm, you see. He can win over the snobbiest people.

'Your brother,' said Henry distantly, 'would have made a good soldier.'

Mr Bullstrode barged in.

'Your majesty!' he cried, half bowing, half bending at the knee as though someone was aiming a blow at his head.

But Henry walked past him without a glance. To the Dean's word of welcome he nodded curtly. The Dean's out-stretched hand was left hanging in the air.

Unruffled and without more ado, the Dean addressed the ghosts:

'Father Benedict, Major André, King Henry of England, we welcome you as representatives of the men and women, famous and obscure, who are buried within the walls of this Abbey. We welcome you also as members of that great company who have passed through death's gloomy portal ...'

When it was Father Benedict's turn to reply he kept it as brief as possible. He didn't mention Jonny.

Mr Bullstrode produced the agreement with a flourish and spread it on the table. The Dean explained that in exchange for Jonny, the Chapter solemnly pledged them-selves and their successors never to open the Abbey to visitors during 'those hours between midnight and dawn that are properly reserved for the exercise and recreation of ghosts'.

The Dean signed for the Abbey and Father Benedict for the ghosts.

'You won't forget the American market, Mr Dean,' Mr Bullstrode hissed, 'the Ambassador is here.'

So Dad had fixed it after all. I was glad for Major André's sake, but I didn't like the look on Henry's face. If Henry lost his temper now, things could go badly wrong.

The granting of Major André's pardon seemed painfully long. The Ambassador droned on about 'healing the wounds of history' whatever that meant. As I had feared, Henry's patience ran out. After a few minutes he strode forward, seized the paper from the Ambassador's hand and tore the pardon in two.

'I'll not spend another thousand years in my grave to satisfy this felon's pride,' he growled.

Mr Bullstrode hurried forward like a head waiter who sees an important guest throw his dinner to the floor, but Henry struck him a back-handed blow across the face knocking him to the ground. Two policemen ran forward and then stopped, obviously uncertain whether Henry of Lancaster was their responsibility.

Henry saw them and drew his sword. The blade flashed in the television lights as he swung the sword above his head with both arms. It was an easy, powerful movement for a man who had not used a sword for five hundred years. I wondered whether he practised every night for something to do.

Henry stood there, ready to strike, daring the living world to come at him.

I heard Father Benedict say, 'If you use that sword, Lancaster, it will not be a thousand years but eternity.'

Slowly, Henry lowered the sword so that his hands were level with his waist and the blade rising above his right shoulder. Further he would not go.

Father Benedict looked at the Dean. They raised their hands together in what could have been a blessing or a farewell. Then the ghosts backed away towards the Great

West Door like men who were no longer certain of their welcome. Major André left the pieces of his pardon on the ground. The crowd was hushed and tense.

'What about Jonny!' I shouted and my words seemed to echo all round the Sanctuary as though it was an empty hall.

The ghosts didn't or couldn't hear. They just kept backing away stiffly. No one else, not even Dad, said or did anything to help.

The Great West Door was opening again to receive the ghosts. I ran forward.

'Hey, what about Jonny?'

One by one the ghosts stepped into the opening and the door began to close. I just got there in time and threw myself against the wood. That checked the closing but all I could see inside was darkness.

'Jonny, where the hell are you?' I cried.

He stepped casually out of the shadows, looking thoroughly pleased with himself and wearing that silly, floppy hat he had pinched from Prince Richard.

'Come on Jonny!'

I could still feel the pressure on the other side of the door and I was furious with him for just standing there as if he had all the time in the world.

'I can't,' he said in an offhand sort of voice.

'Oh brilliant! Why not?'

'Because I'm dead, you ninny. You know I am. You saw me fall.'

Chapter 23

'Did you see him fall?' asked Dr Rosewater.

'I can't remember.'

'Try.'

I stared out of the window. The rain was falling in patches. On the other side of the river the sky was light.

'He's not dead,' I said, without turning round, 'not properly dead anyway.'

'The ghosts cheated you,' he said, 'they cheated us all.'

'That's not true,' I told him, 'they wanted to give Jonny back but the Promotions Board hadn't made up its mind.'

'When will they decide?'

I looked at my watch.

'They might have decided already but I shan't know until midnight. I'll have to climb into the Abbey again.'

'What are the chances?' he asked.

'Pretty good Father Benedict says. Twins are special cases. They bring good luck to the family. So if one dies the Promotions Board usually sends him back.'

I looked out of the window again. Funny how it could be so wet here and so dry across the river. The daffodils on the window-ledges were all dropping now with their heads hanging down over the sides of the boxes.

'How did he fall?' Dr Rosewater asked.

He was sitting on Jonny's bed. When I didn't answer he said: 'You can't bottle it up for ever.'

'He was fooling about,' I said quietly.

'How do you know?'

'I was watching him.'

'But it was dark, wasn't it?'

"I could still see him every time he came to the edge. He shouted, "Hey look Shamus!" and pretended to lose his balance. The time he fell it was the same. He shouted "Hey look Shamus!" I was tired and fed up with looking but I did. He was on the edge waving his arms like a bird to keep his balance but he couldn't. He seemed to jump just as if there was no danger at all. He just dropped straight down.

Dr Rosewater made no comment. After a while he put his hands on his knees ready to go. It was as if he really did not want to know the truth after all. But having started to tell him I wanted to go on.

'He wasn't bleeding,' I said, 'he was just lying between rows of chairs with his legs bent under him. I said something daft like, "Jonny, are you OK?" I didn't touch him. I could see he was unconscious. I remember muttering 'Oh God, I pray he's not dead,' over and over as I ran to the Great West Door and banged on it with my fists. The Night Constable didn't hear. I shouted but nobody came. I called to Jonny as if he could hear. I had to talk to someone. Then I found the block of wood they use to wedge open the East Cloister Door. I climbed up one of the memorials and started smashing windows. They heard me then.'

Dr Rosewater nodded as though he approved.

'That was the good thing,' I went on, 'the Night Constable wasn't angry about the windows or about my being in the Abbey. He took one look at Jonny and went to call the hospital. I sat on one of the chairs a few rows from where Jonny was lying. Almost at once I heard the siren of an ambulance. It grew louder and louder but instead of stopping it went on down Victoria Street and died away. Then it was very quiet and I waited.'

'And now you must wait again,' said Dr Rosewater.

'There's a chance, isn't there?' I said.

'Yes I'm sure there is,' he replied. 'Twins are special cases. You said so yourself.'

I didn't see it coming. He gave no sign. Suddenly, in a different voice he said, 'Whether Jonny comes back or not you've got to break out of this dream world of yours.'

I looked at him blankly.

'Break out of it, Shamus!' he snapped so sharply that I jumped.

I remember thinking, 'No, no yet, I'm not ready,' but I didn't say anything.

He looked so fierce I thought he was going to hit me. When he spoke he sounded out of breath as though the effort to control his anger had exhausted him. He could only manage short sentences. Even so I sensed his anger was unreal. He was just trying it on.

'This game is over,' he said. 'You've got to face reality. All this stuff about ghosts is just fantasy. Jonny fell. That's real. The rest is your imagination.'

I glared at him stubbornly. That's what adults never understand – sometimes the daydreams are more impor- tant to you than what they call reality.

He must have recognized the stubbornness on my face for he sprang up and started shaking me with his hands on my shoulders as though the daydreams would fall out of my ears. I hit him hard in the stomach. I don't think I aimed right. We argue about that at school. Some boys say there's an exact spot and if you hit someone on it he collapses like a shot elephant.

Dr Rosewater stepped back. 'That's better,' he said. 'Now listen to me. You've been a pain in the bloody neck to every- body for the last three weeks. Oh yes, I know there's a good reason but you've cashed in on it. That's got to stop. They've all listened to you, they've all given you a lot of time – the Dean, old Canon Ambrose, the police, everybody. If you ask me they've been too patient with you. I've been too patient with you myself. Mr Bullstrode was probably right: a good kick in the pants at the start would have brought you to your senses. Now you're so hooked on your daydreams you can't tell the difference between them and...' he waved his hand over Jonny's bed, 'what is real.'

He paused a moment before going on.

'If you don't break away now, Shamus, you may never be able to do so. I mean that.'

It was my turn now and I really let rip. I don't know whether I had lost control or was just pretending or a bit of both. I shouted at the top of my voice:

'NO! NOT NOW! NOT UNTIL JONNY'S BACK!'

Mum opened the door. Dr Rosewater told her there was nothing wrong. 'I tried to shock him out of it,' he added, 'it was probably a mistake.'

Mum asked me if I was all right. I didn't reply.

'Do you want any supper, darling?'

I shook my head.

When they had gone I went to the window to check on the rain. If it was falling straight the scaffolding would be kept dry by the corrugated iron, but if the wind was blowing it across, most of the pipes and planks would be slippery.

_____Chapter 24_____

I could smell the ghosts long before I reached the level of the nave. The sweet smell of death must have been stronger when the air was damp.

The nave was crowded as usual. I hated the ugly, stinking mass as much as I liked some of them individually. Thank God, this time they made way, leaving a narrow aisle for me to walk through to the screen. The ghosts were silent and they looked afraid, though not of me surely. I had the feeling too that they were under instructions not to communicate with me in any way though it was unlike Father Benedict to order the ghosts about. I was uneasy, and when I passed under the screen I was really worried. There were no ghosts lounging in the choir-stalls as before.

Beyond the choir they were standing in straight rows in the transepts like a well-drilled congregation at a great service.

The explanation of this change in the ghosts' attitude was soon apparent. At the top of the steps leading to the High Altar stood Henry of Lancaster. There was no doubt that he was in command. Sir Lewis Robbesart, armoured and helmeted as usual, stood at one side and slightly behind the King. There was no sign of Father Benedict or Major André, nor for that matter of any of the other Grand Council members. It was as if Henry had seized power and imprisoned all his rivals.

I looked around for Jonny. It was unlike him not to shout something in greeting. But the only other people near the altar were a group of six men, all in army uniforms of one century or another. They did not look friendly.

I stopped at the bottom of the steps and looked at Henry.

'Where's Jonny?' I asked.

I felt like an African explorer who had arrived at the headquarters of a savage tribe; if I got out alive, let alone rescued my brother, it would be a miracle.

Henry's reply confirmed that fear.

'Your brother is safe,' said he, lifting his arrogant voice over my head so that all the ghosts could hear, 'the Promotions Board have granted him permission to return to life as a twin. But he will remain our prisoner until we are sure the Abbey intend to keep their side of the agreement.'

The bad news followed so soon after the good that I wasn't sure what to feel. Jonny would live, that was the important thing. Even Henry could not defy the Promotions Board for long on that.

'How long...?' I began, but Henry started speaking again, squashing my words under his.

His speech was clearly for the benefit of the ghosts but what he had to say was really depressing. The Promotions Board had condemned the public encounters with living

99

souls, all the more so because it had been seen by millions all over the world. The encounter was not only contrary to all the regulations governing the conduct of dead souls; it was a reckless and irresponsible act. Father Benedict and Major André had been sentenced to perpetual darkness and silence. They would not be allowed to leave their tombs until the end of time. The other members of the Grand Council had been sentenced to a thousand years' darkness and silence, and even then there was no guarantee that their cases would be reviewed. I thought of Sir Cloudesley Shovel who had not seen his wife and children for two hundred years. Now he would have to wait another thousand.

Henry, alone of the Grand Council, had not been punished. He did not give the reason but I could guess. When the Promotions Board started their inquiry, Henry must have sold his friends down the river in return for a pardon. And the Board, determined that there should be no such encounters in the future, had put the turncoat in command. No doubt it had been Henry too who had won a pardon for Sir Lewis so that the crazy knight could help him impose his will upon the other ghosts. So Henry, who was just as guilty as the rest, more guilty really because he had urged violence and had been ready to cut down a living soul with his sword, had escaped all punishment and had been given the power he had always wanted. So much for justice after death, I thought.

'Can I see Jonny?' I asked, when the speech was finished and the parade of ghosts dismissed by Sir Lewis.

'You will see him again when I am satisfied the agreement has been honoured,' Henry replied. 'Tell the Dean that. We are a Christian King. Your brother has nothing to fear unless the Abbey plays false. Meanwhile, if you wish to stay until dawn you are free to do so. Sir Lewis will assign one of his men to keep you company.'

Chapter 25

I had four hours to find Jonny and organize an escape for us both. The task seemed so overwhelming I sank on to the steps in despair. To be defeated at this last moment when Jonny had been given a second chance to live would be a bitter blow.

I did not know where to begin. Jonny could be imprisoned in any one of three thousand graves or he could be shut in one of the many small rooms and chapels round the walls of the Abbey. There was no clue. And even if by some miracle I could discover where he was, it would be virtually impossible to smuggle him out of the building.

The soldier Sir Lewis had chosen to keep an eye on me didn't help. He was a short and broad-shouldered captain with a black-bearded face that gave nothing away except a sort of scowling distrust. His gloomy expression never changed as though it had been set for good at the moment of death. He was a soldier of Waterloo, I would say, his tight red tunic torn from his left shoulder to his hip where a French sword or bullet had ripped him open.

Blackbeard accompanied me wherever I went in the Abbey. The other ghosts treated him with respect and a touch of fear. He represented the new power in the land.

I kept my eyes open for Prince Richard and Prince Edward. It was just possible they would know where Jonny was. But a complete circuit of the Abbey did not discover them. Perhaps they too had been shut away because Henry knew they might help me.

Tired of searching and sick of the stench of so many ghosts I sat down on one of the chairs at the back of the nave. I could have cried out of sheer frustration. The ghastly mob walked round and round like prisoners at exercise. They hardly noticed me but no doubt their orders included no acknowledgment of the living soul. Like a new headmaster determined to make his presence felt, Henry had not taken long to fix his authority on them.

I might have sunk even lower into my depression if a simple ruse had not occurred to me. My spirits rose much higher than the idea deserved but at least it gave me hope.

I stood up, looked carefully at my watch, and then said, 'It's time for me to go.'

It was a feeble enough manoeuvre but it worked. Blackbeard's expression did not change. He accompanied me to the archway leading to the triforium and followed me up the winding stone stair. We walked along the triforium together. Below us the ghosts continued their exercise. Ahead of us an old man was sitting near the edge turning something over in his hands. It was Lord Castlereagh and he was loading a pistol. So he had reached the last resort already. Blackbeard ignored him as a prison guard would ignore a harmless lunatic.

At the foot of the wooden steps leading to the roof I stopped and – over-acting – held out my hand.

'Goodbye, sir.'

He made no attempt either to shake my hand or to follow me up the steps. Once inside the roof I locked the door quickly behind me. With the help of Dad's lamp I worked my way back along the great chamber till I reached the small door that, on my last visit, had almost lured me to my death. This time I took no risks. I knelt on the beams before sliding the bolt back. I did not let the door swing open but controlled its movement by holding the bolt. I peered down through the small opening.

It was a long shot but it was successful. I had gambled that once I was out of the way Jonny would be released. It took me ten minutes to spot him and when I did it was the floppy hat that gave him away. That and the two golden heads walking beside him. It was difficult to tell from this height whether he was being guarded but I had to work on the assumption that he was.

I eased back from the opening and bolted the door. Was the best time to attempt a rescue now, while the Abbey was crowded, or just before dawn when most of the ghosts would have gone to their tombs?

I decided to wait. There was a risk that Jonny might be ordered back to his prison before dawn but it was a risk I would have to take. I made myself as comfortable as possible on the boards between the beams. Every half-hour I would open the door just wide enough to check that Jonny was still there. Knowing him, he would keep on the move so that I should not have to wait too long before he passed below me. I wondered whether escape was on his mind too. I guessed that the new régime of Henry of Lancaster had dampened his enthusiasm for life after death.

Though I had plenty of time to work out a plan, I could think of nothing more ingenious than trying to attract Jonny's attention from the triforium so that he could make a dash for the winding stair. We only needed a head start. Once in the roof we could lock the door behind us and climb out of the window on to the battlements. In the open air we would be safe. No ghost would dare to leave the Abbey now, especially at dawn.

I told myself that simple plans were usually the best. That calmed my nerves as the hour approached.

At a quarter-past four I checked the scene below. There were so few ghosts around I feared I might already be too late. I hurried back along the roof and slowly and quietly unlocked the door at the other end. The first thing I saw was Lord Castlereagh still sitting on the triforium floor holding the pistol in his lap. The anxiety I felt on seeing him died quickly when I realized he was asleep. I put Dad's lamp on the floor, and leaving the door ajar, went on tiptoe down the wooden steps. I crept past Castlereagh's back, keeping close to the wall so that I would be out of sight of any ghosts on the other side of the nave who happened to look up. Near the head of the winding stairs I lay down and eased myself across the triforium to look down into the nave.

Jonny and the two princes were standing right in front of me by the Unknown Warrior's tomb. A khaki figure was talking to them.

In my excitement I jumped to the wrong conclusions. I assumed the Unknown Warrior would be friendly and I assumed that as there were no other ghosts nearby Jonny was unguarded. Like a fool I stood up and shouted:

'Jonny! Up here quick.'

Thank God he saw me straightaway and for once in his life didn't argue. It was the first moment that I was sure he wanted to come back. I saw him leap forward but not quickly enough. The Unknown Warrior seized his arm so that Jonny was forced to spin round and grapple with him. The princes came to Jonny's rescue. They sprang on the soldier's back like leopards, dragging him down. Jonny wrenched his arm free and ran for the stairs to the triforium. But my shout and the few seconds delay as Jonny wrestled with the Unknown Warrior had blown any chances of a clean getaway.

Jonny reached Lord Salisbury's tomb only two strides ahead of Blackbeard, who must have been on guard though out of sight, and the Unknown Warrior who had easily shaken off the princes. Sir Lewis appeared from my left and gave chase too.

That was the end of my grandstand view. I looked back to check that the door to the roof was still open and only half noticed that Lord Castlereagh was on his feet. We could still make it if Jonny was quick.

As soon as his head appeared, I cried, 'Come on!' and started towards the wooden steps. But I had under-estimated the ghosts. One of them had caught Jonny's ankle.

'Hey, Shamus. He's pulling me down.'

By the time I had run back to him, Blackbeard had both Jonny's legs trapped in an armlock. Jonny was clinging to the rope that acted as a handrail and was trying to wriggle himself free but it was obvious he could not weaken the Captain's iron grip. The only good thing was that Sir Lewis and the Unknown Warrior could do nothing to make the situation worse because they were blocked by the sharp twist of the spiral.

I looked round for something to throw at Blackbeard's head but there was nothing, not a single object of any use. While Jonny yelled at me and swore at Blackbeard in language that would have given Dad a heart attack, I was seized with a paralysing numbness. My brain seemed unable to give any instructions to my limbs. I just stood there helplessly as Jonny's hands began to slip down the rope.

The explosion so close to my head made my ears ring. I must have jumped aside and looked back at the same time for I still have a clear picture of Lord Castlereagh with his straight right arm holding the smoking pistol. The ball had hit Blackbeard in the chest. He could not die again and he had no blood to shed but the force of the blow knocked him back so that he had to release his grip on Jonny.

Jonny was up and over the top step and ducking under Castlereagh's arm before I could recover my wits. Now it was Jonny who was shouting 'Come on!'

I looked at Lord Castlereagh but his eyes were set on some distant point. What did he care about Henry's wrath? Then I looked back at the stairs. Sir Lewis and the Unknown Warrior were trying to heave Blackbeard out of their path and were obviously still intent on pursuit.

I reached the wooden steps as Jonny was going through the door into the roof. 'He's safe now,' I thought, 'they can't catch him.' I sprang through the door and slammed it after me, turning the key in the lock as the wood banged into place.

'Did you bring a light?' Jonny asked quickly.

I bent down and felt on the floor, but as I did so something struck the door such a blow the wood cracked. I remembered Sir Lewis's mailed fist. We were not safe yet. A second blow sounded even more powerful.

We left the lamp and stumbled across the floor guided only by the faint light shed by the window.

We reached the window just as we heard the door crash down behind us. Jonny went first and then helped me up through the narrow opening. The air was cold and the wind from the river washed our hot cheeks. We walked along the gutter as fast as we dared and then stepped out on to the scaffolding. From the direction of the window I heard a terrible cry that faded almost at once as though someone had promptly turned down the volume. I don't know what caused that frightening sound and I had no intention of going back then to find out. But my guess is that Sir Lewis, his vision narrowed by the slit in his helmet, had not seen us scrambling through the window; and that instead he had found the small door that swings away from you when you pull back the bolt and draws you after it into space.

Ahead of us the sky across the Thames was already pale.

'Look Jonny,' I said, as he started to climb down in front of me.

He laughed that horse laugh of his.

'Hey Shamus,' he cried, loud enough to wake the dead, 'we made it!'

Chapter 26

It was a hot summer evening three months later. The setting sun was hidden by a haze and the air was heavy and still. With any luck there would be a storm.

Jonny was trying out his crutches on the green in Dean's Yard. He had been in a wheel-chair for a month after leaving hospital. Guess who had to push him around? At first Mum wouldn't let him out of her sight but after a week or two it was, 'Shamus dear, why don't you take Jonny to St James's Park', or, 'Jonny, if you want to go to the river I'm sure Shamus will take you.'

Jonny sat in his wheel-chair like a prince. With his plastered legs stuck out in front of him and his head still bandaged he was the wounded hero too. Old ladies would stop us in the street to ask how Jonny was getting on, and the man who sells evening papers outside Scotland Yard stood to attention and saluted every time I pushed Jonny past. 'They're twins you know,' I heard him say to his next customer.

Jonny lapped it all up but I thanked God when the doctor told him to start practising on his crutches.

'Hey look Shamus,' he said as he managed a turn. His left leg was still in plaster and his toes stuck out of the end. His right leg which had only been broken in two places was almost healed so that he could put nearly his whole weight on it.

He tried a few more steps and then collapsed on to the grass with a whistle.

Somewhere to the east above the Abbey roof the sky flashed.

'Oh brilliant!' cried Jonny, 'there's going to be a storm.'

But there was no thunder. We stretched out on the grass gazing up at the darkening sky.

Jonny had recovered consciousness in the early morning of April 25th. The doctors at the hospital said it was a miracle. He had been in a coma for three and a half weeks. Jonny claimed that it was a record but it wasn't. I checked in the *Guinness Book of Records.*

'It's a record for a boy of my age,' he assured me.

The hospital rang Dad. I remembered hearing the telephone ringing. I went with Mum and Dad to the hospital. Dawn was just breaking but the street lights were still on. We weren't allowed to stay long. Jonny was lying on his back. He recognized us all right but he couldn't remember at first what had happened. The nurse said the first thing he asked for was food. That's typical Jonny. He has this theory that you ought to eat whenever you can because you never know when the world's food supply is going to run out.

I visited him every day in hospital. He had his own colour television and always seemed to be surrounded by fresh bowls of fruit. When he was allowed to sit up we played backgammon. We didn't talk much about the accident, though he did ask me what I had done when he 'conked out'.

'You're lucky to be alive,' I told him.

He looked pretty thoughtful at that, pretty thoughtful for Jonny that is.

I never said a word about my own adventures. Dr Rosewater still came to see me twice a week but there was no need. I knew I had been living in a dream world. That wasn't a crime. And I didn't need him to tell me that it was all because I couldn't face the possibility that Jonny might never recover.

He wasn't a bad doctor as doctors go. When he saw that his job was done he cut down his visits to one every two weeks. We talked about anything but ghosts, but on his last visit he asked: 'No more ghosts?'

'No more ghosts,' I replied, and we laughed together at the very thought.

I stood on the landing and watched him go downstairs with Dad. At the front door he said, 'Let me know if there's any recurrence. I don't think there will be, not now his brother's back.'

Dad held out his hand and said goodbye.

The thunder-clap struck without warning. Jonny was up on his crutches so fast I wondered whether the old fraud hadn't been capable of walking for weeks. We hurried back to the house expecting the first raindrops to hit us any minute. But it was nearly two hours before the storm broke. Then the rain really bombed down, so hard it was bouncing up again off the pavements and the roofs. We left the bedroom curtains open so that we could watch.

We were both in bed when Dad came in. It must have been ten o'clock or thereabouts. He was wearing gumboots.

'Shamus, have you seen my map-reading lamp?' he asked.

I said 'No,' without thinking but after he had gone I remembered.

I lay still.

Just for a few seconds my heart froze. But then I laughed at myself. 'Grip, Shamus, grip!' Dad must have lost the lamp somewhere. It wasn't even a coincidence. People lost things the whole time.

The storm rumbled away across the river and the force went out of the rain. But with the lights off we could still see the sheet lightning against the clouds.

Jonny said quietly, 'I know where Dad's lamp is.'

'Where?' I asked him, secretly relieved that someone knew.

'It's where you left it,' he replied, 'by the door in the Abbey roof.'

I turned on him.

'What the hell are you talking about, Jonny?'

He didn't even look at me. He just lay there with a knowing smile on his face.

I sprang out of bed.

'What did you mean?' I said, trying to keep my voice calm.

'Actually, I shouldn't have said that,' was his reply.

'But you did.'

'Did I? I can't remember.'

He was at his most infuriating.

'You said the lamp was by the door in the Abbey roof where I left it. Isn't that what you said?'

'Perhaps I did. So what?'

'It couldn't be,' I told him, 'I've never been in the Abbey roof. That's what.'

He looked at me then.

'Hey Shamus,' he said, 'we've got to keep this to ourselves. That was the condition. I could tell you but no one else.'

'Tell me what?' I demanded.

'That twins are special cases,' he replied, 'that's why I was allowed to come back.'

I realized then that in some way I did not understand he had shared my adventures. 'Funny things, twins,' Dr Rosewater had said. Jonny's mind must have been plugged into mine even though he was unconscious. That's just like him. He lies there snoozing while I do all the work.

As I got back into bed, I said: 'You weren't allowed to come back. I rescued you.'

'Oh, come on, Shamus!' he cried as though it was impossible to imagine that he would ever need my help.

It was my turn to smile to myself. I had saved him because my will had been stronger than his. He had been drawn towards the world of ghosts but I had pulled him

110

back. In the long struggle between our minds, I had won.

'I can't think why I bothered,' I said aloud.

'Because you couldn't do without me,' he replied laughing.

I couldn't help laughing too. He took everything for granted. You could save his life and he would make you feel grateful to him. He was born like that.

Our laughter must have reached Dad down the corridor because he called out, 'Quiet you two!'

'Hey Dad,' Jonny shouted back, 'did you find the lamp?'

'Yes thanks, it was in the car. Now go to sleep.'

But we didn't. Not that night. Not for a long time.